SONS BUILDING

ON THE FATHER'S VISION

"It was in my father's heart to build a house for God."

BY

ALIDI JOHN MPATEYA

DEDICATION

This book is dedicated to the kingdom of God and to all the children of God serving in the Body of Christ as a resource tool for Kingdom advancement.

Table of Contents

FOREWORD

PREFACE

FOREWORD

Sons Building the Fathers' Vision is the book that focuses on obedience and faith. This theme runs throughout the book and the author draws examples from the beginning of the Bible during the time of Adam to the time of the great prophets such as Moses, Joshua, David and Solomon down to the time of Jesus Christ and to the apostles.

But one might ask why should sons build on their fathers' vision? The word "vision" is actually used metaphorically to denote "to carry out the will or wishes or to act on the advice of the father." And the word "father" is broadly used to encompass "spiritual fathers", those who strengthen you in difficult times, complement what you do and provide mentorship. Hence, spiritual fathers include both men and women. According to the author, "spiritual fathering is a bible order which provide spiritual accountability."

In portraying how the sons build the vision of their fathers, Dr. Mpateya looks at the father-son relationship from two angles. On one hand, he talks about biological fathers. In this category, he talks about David and his son Solomon or Abraham and Jacob. On the other hand, he talks about father-son relationship in the spiritual realm. He gives an example of Moses and Joshua, Paul and Timothy, God and Jesus and indeed God and the whole mankind through Jesus Christ. To him, whether the instructions are given by biological fathers or spiritual fathers it makes no difference. What is important is to obey the instructions and implement the task that one has been commissioned to do. Moreover, the sons do not necessarily have to have experience to do the task before them, but the blessings they receive from their father are adequate.

According to Mpateya, there are obvious benefits that are to be reaped from carrying out the will of the father while dire consequences also await those who do not implement the father will. The fall of Adam and Cain's failure to please God with his offering are classic examples. Hence, the message is very clear about those who fail to build on their fathers' vision. However, for the vision to be carried out communication is vital. Mpateya places great value in communicating the right message to the person to implement the vision. Communication is therefore key to the success of the assignment.

Although Sons Building the Fathers' Vision has a Christian message and draws examples from the Bible, its theme has a universal applicability. It applies to the youth and adults, Christians and non-Christians. Those who listen and are obedient to the God and the youth who obey their fathers will succeed in life. Hence, the audience and theme go beyond Christianity. The book challenges the readers to assess whether they are following God's will or whether their lives are right with God.

Mpateya writes the book in a simple and straightforward language. This makes reading easy and the book accessible to everyone. Once you start reading the book you cannot help but read more to find out what the vision is all about. The arrangement of the chapters makes the reader follow the theme from one chapter to the other with any difficulty.

Sons Building the Fathers' Vision is a book that should be read by everyone who wants to know how obedience and faith produce the right results. It is also a source of comfort to those who do not have biological fathers to guide them. Spiritual fathers will equally give them the much-needed support for them to succeed provided they listen, obedient and act. It is through spiritual fathers that blessings from God flow.

Neville Goldman
(Ebenezer International)

PREFACE

The Christian religion is more than a religion; it is a relationship. Religion is defined in many ways. One explanation is as a personal belief in God, and trying to reach Him. However Christianity is not the people reaching God, but rather Christ first reaching them. Therefore if one believes in Jesus the Christ he becomes part of the family. Jesus came to establish a relationship that allows all believers to become members of the household of faith. That's making them part of him as a brother.

No longer do I call you servants; for the servant knoweth not what his lord doeth: but I have called you friends; for all things that I heard from my Father, I have made known unto you. (John 15:15)

The scripture below is clear on the fact that all believers are not identified on the basis of their race or culture. Christianity therefore transcends cultural and traditional norms, as all nations are incorporated under God. It integrates all believers in Jesus the Christ regardless of their background.

There can be neither Jew nor Greek, there can be neither bond nor free, there can be no male and female; for ye all are one man in Christ Jesus. (Galatians 3:28)

In the spiritual realm there is no gender differentiation. In Christ we are all sons of God. The examples that I have used in this book do not seek to discriminate against females, because in the spiritual realm all are sons. In the kingdom of God male and female will function equally and harmoniously.

For ye received not the spirit of bondage again unto fear; but ye received the spirit of adoption, whereby we cry, Abba, Father. (Romans 8:15)

One obtains a new birthright and identity upon coming to Jesus the Christ, which then enables him to relate with God as a son. God through His foreknowledge had purposed to restore back the fallen man, so that He can relate with him to the praise of His Glory.

"To wit, that God was in Christ reconciling the world unto himself, not reckoning unto them their trespasses, and having committed unto us the word of reconciliation." (1 Corinthians 5:19)

Even Jesus emphasized that his mission on earth was based on advancing the kingdom of his Father. His vision was from his Father, he came because of it, he gave all his life to fulfill and complete it as a faithful Son.

I can of mine own self do nothing: as I hear, I judge: and my judgment is just; because I seek not mine own will, but the will of the father which hath sent me. (John 5:30)

This book also seeks to address principles that affect relationships between fathers and sons. The importance of a spiritual father and son relationship is highlighted. Although the title of this book is "Sons building on the Father's Vision", it does not seek to discriminate women, as previously mentioned, in the gender aspect.

If we take a journey on studying the Bible and the people who became successful, including Solomon, we come to the conclusion that they were properly fathered. In the case of Solomon all his achievements and success can be traced back to the fact that he was well connected with his father. It was in that posture that he was equipped with everything necessary that made it possible for him to fulfill his vision.

The book of Malachi speaks of the turning of the hearts of the fathers back to their sons and the sons to their fathers. It emphasizes that it is through the turning of hearts of fathers to their sons or vice versa that the land will avoid being cursed.

Behold, I will send you Elijah the prophet before the

great and terrible day of Jehovah come. And he shall turn the heart of the fathers to the children, and the heart of the children to their fathers; lest I come and smite the earth with a curse. (Malachi 4:5, 6)

We live in a fatherless generation, and unless God raises up spiritual fathers, the land will be cursed. The key to true spiritual blessings will only be found in a father and son spiritual relationship. As it is stated in this scripture that the spirit of Elijah was coming back, it is important to note that Elijah is the only person in the Bible who gives us a picture of what spiritual fathering is. Even though Elisha was not his biological son, he gave him a spiritual inheritance of a double portion which in return enabled him to accomplish twice the work or success Elijah did.

And it came to pass, when they were gone over, that Elijah said unto Elisha, Ask what I shall do for thee, before I be taken away from thee. And Elisha said, I pray thee, let a double portion of thy spirit be upon me. And he took the mantle of Elijah that fell from him, and smote the waters, and said, Where is the LORD God of Elijah? and when he also had smitten the waters, they parted hither and thither: and Elisha went over. (2 Kings 2:9, 14)

There were sixteen miracles that Elijah performed during his earthly ministry and there are thirty two miracles that Elisha performed in his earthly ministry. This can give us an indication of what can happen when one walks under a spiritual father. The results will double as was in the case of Elisha. I believe God wants his children to be successful and to be great achievers. Hence the last book of the Old Testament closes with a strong prophetic message pointing to the coming of the spirit of Elijah, which is the "spirit of fathering". I believe there are great fathers today that God has raised up; they are both male and female. It will be of great advantage for everyone to be under true spiritual covering.

It is my prayer therefore that as you read through this book, you will find the importance of being fathered, the joys and the benefits thereof.

CHAPTER 1

THE VALUE OF COMMUNICATION

Solomon's father, David, had a vision to build a house for God. However, David understood prophetic order: In order to accomplish something in God there is a need to be connected with the spiritual voice that will provide prophetic insight. He then communicated his vision to a prophet for spiritual input and approval.

Now it came to pass, as David sat in his house, that David said to Nathan the prophet, Lo, I dwell in an house of cedars, but the ark of the covenant of the LORD remaineth under curtains. Then Nathan said unto David, Do all that is in thine heart; for God is with thee. (1 Chronicles 17:1-2)

Let us look at this picture of David, now settled on his throne as King of Israel. He did not get complete satisfaction from occupying the highest office in the Land. He then sought for something that would cause him to be satisfied and settled as a leader of God's people. The scripture above indicates that David had a dialogue with Prophet Nathan. And in his dialogue with Prophet Nathan, he eluded to the fact that he was quite settled in his house made of cedars, however he was dissatisfied with the ark of the Lord dwelling under curtains. Nathan perceived that this was a heart issue and then responded to David with the counsel that said, do what is in your heart God is with you. David's heart longed for the ark of the Lord to come to a place where he was. When David became the King the ark was not in the midst of the people of God. Therefore, the first thing that he did was to bring the ark of the covenant of the Lord to Jerusalem. His first attempt to bring it to Jerusalem was not successful. He had to learn through trial and error and got his success at his second attempt. His determination paid off. Sometimes we try and fail, but as long as we are determined to do something, it always pays off. There may be some causality in the process, but as long as you do not give up and dare to be different you'll see the fruits of your labor. In David's case for instance, somebody died in the process of bringing back the Ark of the Lord. It is at this point that after the Ark of the Lord had stayed for many years in the temporary shelter that David wanted to take it to the next level. The key of taking the Ark of the Covenant of the Lord is communication. He communicated that to the prophet that he wanted the Ark of the Covenant of the Lord to be to housed in a proper building instead of it being in a shelter. He wanted a kingdom with the glory.

It is important to note that God even referred to David as a man after His own heart. The heart of David was for the presence of God. The Ark represented the glory of God; hence Jesus is also referred to as the greater David. Jesus is the King of glory; David wanted to reign with the glory. As the scripture declares:

As the deer pants for streams of water, so my soul pants for you, my God. (Psalm 42:1 NIV)

David's concern when he reasoned with the prophet was that the Ark of the Lord remained under curtains. Hence, he wanted to build a dwelling place for the Ark of the Covenant of the Lord. One would say he had a right motive. His motivation was to see a place which had quartered the presence of God where nations could come and worship. This was the vision that was burning in David's heart. He had a vision. Everything begins with a vision.

And the LORD answered me, and said, "Write the vision, and make it plain upon tables, that he may run that readeth it." (Habakkuk. 2:2)

IMPORTANT ASPECTS OF THE VISION

- A) The vision must be put in writing
- B) It must be made clear so that it might be understood by those that are responsible for implementing it - or runners, so to speak
- C) It must have an origin

David handed over an original vision to his son Solomon as written in the following scripture.

Now, my son, the LORD be with thee; and prosper thou, and build the house of the LORD thy God, as he hath said of thee. (I Chronicles 22:11)

This is supported by the fact that says when Solomon finalized the project of building the temple which housed the ark of the Covenant of the Lord, he acknowledged the author of the vision, his father.

Now it was in the heart of my father David to build a house for the name of the LORD, the God of Israel. (I Kings 8:17)

He was just a son fulfilling his father's project. The kingdom of God is a family affair that receives a vision and the vision is passed on from one generation to the next, as entailed in this scripture:

Jesus saith unto him, "Have I been so long time with you, and yet hast thou not known me, Philip? He that hath seen me hath seen the Father; and how sayest thou then, Show us the Father?" (John 14:9)

Jesus said, what I see my Father do is what I do. The kingdom of God operates from the premises of son-ship. It's the relationship from the Father to the son. It is not a democracy, father and son in relationship.

For though ye have ten thousand instructors in Christ, yet have ye not many fathers: for in Christ Jesus I have begotten you through the gospel. (I Corinthians 4:15)

This statement may also serve as a parallel truth; Even if one has many church members, not all of them are sons.

SUPPORT SYSTEMS

Salvation comes with everything. It is a complete package. Jesus' own words said:

The thief cometh not, but for to steal, and to kill, and to destroy: I am come that they might have life, and that they might have it more abundantly. (John 10:10)

His finished work of the cross provided everything that was required to deal with every aspect of life. Every predicament that caused mankind to suffer He took upon Himself in order to pay the ultimate price through His sacrificial death. He even declared it is finished. In His vision he incorporated everything that pertains to life, in His body he took all sickness, all poverty and all our limitations. God is not exclusive in His dealings. He design is not only limited to family members. He incorporates outsiders when need be. Below is a typical case of how He incorporated people from a distant land to come and connect with His Son from His birth. They came to celebrate and to partner with Him as seen in the scripture below.

For unto you is born this day in the city of David a Saviour, which is Christ the Lord. (Luke 2:11)

Key people, well-to-do people from the business world, were connected to the vision of God's son for two reasons: To provide a financial support system — divine provision for the vision. From the birth of Jesus, the Son of God, business people were attached to His ministry or vision to provide financial assistance for His vision. Vision can be resisted from the onset as seen in the instance where King Herod ordered the assassination of little children that were born at the same time as Jesus. This was an attempt to eliminate the emerging of Jesus. Vision always suffers opposition, hence God always provides angelic accompaniment to protect and safeguard His visionaries. Vision attracts people from near and far with resources, provision and manpower.

As with the birth of Jesus, wise and wealthy men had a holy mandate to finance Jesus' ministry from His first days on Earth. They left their businesses in haste to go and meet the King that was born that day, according to the angel. God did not send the reigning king of the time, King Herod; rather He sent wealthy businessmen; a group of business representatives. As a matter of fact, when King Herod heard about Jesus, he wanted to kill him.

This group of God-chosen business representatives was not bothered about the distance, time and cost. Rather they were enthused and honored to go and see, first hand, this miracle that God had brought to the earth. Was it possible that God was seeking to empower his Son through these rich men, as well as wanting to bless their businesses through this experience?

It would be fair to say, that if wealthy people of this magnitude were to have such a meeting with a king, they would not come empty handed. In this case they brought with them a substantial number of gifts as it is stated in the scripture passages below. They brought Him gold and precious gifts and expensive merchandise.

And when they were come into the house, they saw the young child with Mary his mother, and fell down, and worshipped him: and when they had opened their treasures, they presented unto him gifts; gold, and frankincense and myrrh. (Matthew 2:11)

I suggest that these gifts could have become the initial capital in Jesus ministry bank account. Furthermore, this would have given Jesus a boost financially in the initial years of His life on earth. Even as God's Son there is nothing that could have stopped God from using people to provide for His Son financially.

We also read about the angelic involvement surrounding His birth and the announcing of His birth. This further suggests that God had ordained angelic ministry for His Son whilst on earth for two reasons: as angels ministering to Him and also to provide protection.

Let's now look at important parallels between this story and the story of David and Solomon. In looking at David and his son Solomon, we will find out that David also made provision for Solomon and gave him everything necessary for him to build the house of God. The first parallel: Solomon and Jesus both received a vision from their fathers. They both had a clear definition of their mission on earth from their fathers.

Jesus in his own words said,

"I came to do my Father's will and finish it." (John 4:34)

He also said the following,

So Jesus replied, "Truly, truly, I tell you, the Son can do nothing by Himself, unless He sees the Father doing it. For whatever the Father does, the Son also does." (John 5:19)

This makes it clear that Jesus had a mandate from his father. They both received a blue print from their fathers.

I have worked hard to provide materials for building the Temple of the LORDfour thousand tons of gold, nearly forty thousand tons of silver, and so much iron and bronze that it cannot be weighed. I have also gathered lumber and stone for the walls, though you may need to add more. You have many skilled stonemasons and carpenters and craftsmen of every kind available to you. They are expert goldsmiths and silversmiths and workers of bronze and iron. Now begin the work, and may the LORD be with you! (1 Chronicles 22:14 –, NLT).

The second parallel between the circumstances surrounding the birth and mission of Jesus and that of David and Solomon is that both were given assistance by way of manpower and material resources from their fathers.

Through the appearance of the star, the wise men from the east were given specific direction to how they would find Jesus, the newly born King. Not only where he was, but also who he was, so as for them to properly prepare a kingly gift. The message they received was that a king was born in Bethlehem.

And when they come into the house, they saw the young child with Mary his mother, and fell down, and worshipped him: and when they had opened their treasures, they presented unto him gifts; gold, and frankincense, and myrrh. (Matthew 2:11)

I would like to suggest here that these high profile, wise, business men would not have gone to the lengths they did, just to see a new baby, but rather they had been given a revelation that the King had been born, and that is who they knew they were going to see. Their motivation for coming was the fact that they were coming to see a king, not a baby. Their gift said it all. They did not bring diapers or baby food, but gold, frankincense, and myrrh… these were precious, extravagant, and the most expensive of gifts.

When God wants to build His work He will connect the right people together, at the right times, who have the right qualifications for what he wants to accomplish.

Throughout Jesus' ministry He was surrounded by those who came from all sectors of life, including the business world. Those who were actively involved in Jesus' ministry included Matthew the tax collector; Peter the fisherman; Zacchaeus the tax collector; Luke the beloved physician; Judas the accountant and treasurer; and Mary Magdalene, a woman who was healed by Jesus and who was a part of the group of women who had and used their material resources to care for the needs of Jesus as well as his disciples. These women took care of the ministry in practical ways and also financed their journeys. (See John 19:25; 20:1-18; Luke 8:1-3; 23:49, 55-56; 24:1-11; Mark 15:40-41, 47; 16:1-11; Matthew 27:55-56, 61; 28:1-10).

The Scripture that we read earlier tells us that David told Solomon that he had prepared hundreds of thousands of tons of gold, tons of silver, iron, and an abundance of wood and stones, as well as workmen.

Jesus and Solomon both had a blue print. We shall call it a 'building plan'. Here we find yet another parallel between the two, over and above the building plan, which had everything provided for them. A common resource we find in both stories is gold. Gold was part of their kingdom blessing and in both stories, it speaks of royal provision. Gold also portrayed excellence. The way they carried out their work was excellent.

At the conclusion of Jesus' ministry on the earth He prayed this prayer to His father requesting Him to glorify Him:

After Jesus said this, He looked towards heaven "Father, the hour has come. Glorify your Son, that your Son may glorify you." (John 17:1)

It is interesting to note that after carrying out His vision in the manner that was handed over to Him by His Father, Jesus finished His work in a glorious manner. And the writer of the book of Philippians has this to say about the glorified Jesus Christ:

Wherefore God also hath highly exalted him and given him a name which is above every name: That at the name of Jesus every knee should bow, of things in heaven, and things on earth and things under the earth. (Philippians 2:9-10)

And after Solomon had completed the Temple and brought the Ark of the Covenant into it, the glory of the Lord fell, as we read in 1 Kings 8:10-11, and so filled the house that the priests could not continue ministering. Solomon became one of the greatest and wisest kings that ever lived. The scriptures make this clear:

Wisdom and knowledge is granted unto thee; and I will give thee riches, and wealth, and honor, such as none of the kings have had that have been before thee, neither shall there be any after thee have the like. (2 Chronicles 1:12)

There is a treasure hidden in the subject of communication and happy are they that find it. I feel much time must be invested in this subject, and much digging must be done to discover this hidden treasure. This is one of the subjects that form a great part of our humanity and our mandate as believers; therefore it cannot be ignored.

Good communication skills play a great part in all spheres of life. It is through good communication skills that successful business people, athletes, and prosperous people in the world at large, became successful. Advertisements of different products that are aired on television, and through other means such as billboards and flyers, are all part of communication. Companies that advertise do so to communicate their product or service to their consumers.

COMMUNICATION MUST BE CLEAR

One day I gave an instruction that was not very clear and it cost me very dearly. I asked one of my spiritual daughters to iron my pants and shirt. Those were my favorite clothes, and they included a beautiful Howard university t-shirt that was given to me by Bishop Wellington Boone. I gave this message in a native language. I wanted my daughter to iron my clothes and she interpreted what I said as she must 'burn them'. Taking them outside the house, she lit a match on them and they were gone. After taking a bath, I asked for my clothes, but they were now just a heap of ashes. Upon asking her for my clothes, she replied, "You told me to burn them". There was nothing I could do that was going to change the result. My clothes were gone, my beautiful t-shirt and my pants were now ashes.

This story shows that there was a serious breakdown of communication. One of the primary responsibilities of parenthood is good communication. This is one of the most important and essential elements of life that prepares children for their future.

The quality and progress in children's lives are dependent upon the information that is communicated to them from the ground roots by their parents. Therefore the level of communication from the parental point of view is absolutely essential and vital, for the future of the children depends on it.

Communication is the basis of life, without it life is meaningless and abnormal. Communication forms the backbone of every community. Much time must be dedicated to communication, for without it there will be no society. Just imagine a life without proper communication channels such as postal services, telecommunication and internet, newspaper, books, radio, etc.

Occasionally you may need to talk or write to your friends that are far away. You may need information about what is happening in other parts of the world. Sometimes you want to listen to a tune on the radio. All these forms of communication make life easier and more bearable.

There have been some major breakthroughs in our modern technology in the area of communication. Distance is no longer a limitation. One can communicate with people a million miles away and be able to hear them clearly, and this can happen in a matter of seconds. Through electronic media, communication has been made easy. Newspaper companies are cashing in everyday, making a great fortune by providing information. Yes, we are surely living in the communication age.

Cellular phone companies likewise are not leaving any stone unturned. Mobile handsets are being upgraded more often than we can keep up with, and the designers and manufacturers are catering for every need. This means you can now listen to the radio, or watch television, on the mobile set as well as have your music and video clips on the same set.

The forth generation cellular phone network is able to transmit live data through video clips; you are able to see the person you are talking to regardless of distance. This forth generation transmission is quite advanced, it cannot compare with the second generation; it allows you more band speed thereby enabling you to transmit more data per minute more efficiently.

COMMUNICATION BRIGHTENS THE FUTURE

Where there is proper communication the future is bright and secure. Let's take for instance a marriage that lacks communication. That relationship is bound to fail. When national leaders cease to communicate, there will be anarchy and confusion.

Train up a child in a way he should go, when he is old he will not depart from it. (Proverbs 22:6)

The Bible says that a child must be raised up in such a way that when he grows up he will not depart from that way. It is one's upbringing that one exhibits in life. A person must be equipped with proper principles and the foundations of life that in turn will bring establishment.

In the Bible we are given the account of God's approval on Abraham's life. This is what God had to say in regard to Abraham.

For I know that he will command his children and his household after him and they shall keep the way of the Lord to do justice and judgment, that the Lord may bring upon Abraham that which he has spoken of him. (Genesis 18:19)

Therefore God was not ashamed to call him friend. God takes pleasure in seeing someone who has such outstanding qualities and who devotes so much of his time and effort raising his children to walk in his footsteps with such godly principles. In whatever Abraham did, he was purposefully investing for future generations.

One would say he was far sighted because he was thinking generationally. Therefore what he taught can be regarded as empowerment for those that were coming through his blood line.

God is a friend of communicators because he is a God of communication. This can be traced back to the early days of creation In how he dealt with the first man Adam. He told him:

You may eat the fruit of any tree in the garden, except the tree that gives knowledge of what is good and what is bad. You must not eat the fruit of that tree; if you do, you will die the same day. (Genesis 2:16, 17)

Upon creating Adam, he communicated to him and gave him a copy of His first constitution. This outlined all the do's and don'ts. Allow me to say, Adam had a black and white copy of everything that was expected of him; therefore ignorance was no excuse for any of his actions. When he blew it he knew exactly what he was supposed to have done even though he tried to shift the blame.

When God confronted him after he broke His command he gave the following excuse:

But it was the woman you gave me who brought me the fruit, and I ate it. (Genesis 3:12 NLT)

In his heart of hearts he knew exactly what to do, when to do it, how to do it and where to do it, for God had communicated this to him.

Surely the Lord God does nothing unless He reveals His secret to His servants the prophets. (Amos 3:7 NKJV)

God does nothing unless he first reveals it to his servants, the prophets. What God reveals he expects to be carried out in complete obedience even by generations to come.

How great are his signs! And how mighty are his wonders! His kingdom is an everlasting kingdom, and his dominion is from generation to generation. (Daniel 4:3)

His kingdom is an everlasting one, his dominion is from generation to generation. He raises a people of dominion who will pass dominion to the future generations. Good communicators are those who can leave a legacy. They often focus on raising successors. They are always looking for a generation that will continue from where they left off.

Their departure is not their end. The sign of true fathers is that their lives can be reflected and seen through the lives of their sons.

In the beginning God communicated through His word and spoke the world into existence.

Then God said, "Let there be light," and there was light. (Genesis 1:3 NLT)

There is nothing that existed from anywhere; in other words nothing came into existence without God's word. God established everything through the words He spoke. All creation is a result of what was spoken, or communicated, and it continues to function within the perimeters of His spoken word.

It is quite interesting to note that even the whole of creation communicates in one way or another.

The heavens tell of the glory of God. The skies display his marvelous craftsmanship. Day after day they continue to speak; night after night they make him known. They speak without a sound or a word; their voice is silent in the skies. (Psalm 68:1-3)

Without communication this world would not be what it is today.

God, who in sundry times and diverse manners spoke in times past unto the fathers by the prophets, hath in these days spoken unto us by His Son, whom he hath appointed heir of all things, by whom also he made the worlds. (Hebrews 1:1-2)

What we are learning here is that God is a God of communication. This scripture reveals the God who speaks in a variety of ways. It shows that not only is He a communicator, but His art of communication is diverse. He does not fall short of methods of communicating Himself. He uses diverse ways, many approaches in different places, in different ways He has spoken. Allow me to say He has a communication department that seeks to herald His agenda to all humankind. Therefore His purpose of speaking is to make known His mind, will, plans, and purpose to all of His people.

Today God continues to speak to us through His Son. In the above scripture it is written that God spoke through the prophets and now He is speaking through his Son prophetically, via his body, the church. The church is a prophetic representation of what God is saying currently. God's business on earth is in motion; His representatives receive signals on a continuous basis for the purpose of equipping them to function as His proper representatives. Through all His different means of communication God wants to implement and establish His eternal Kingdom.

There is a classic story in the Bible found in the book of Jeremiah 35:1-15, which deals with this aspect of communication: It reveals the power that comes out of a proper system of communication. Detailed ways of communication help the hearer to understand and enables the person to apply and put into action the communicated principles without struggling.

In the word of God we find this example from the book of Jeremiah. What this story seeks to illustrate to the Israelites is that they had a communication problem in comparison to the tribe of the Rechabites who understood their parents and did what they were told.

The word which came unto Jeremiah from the Lord in the days of Jehoiakim the son of Josiah king of Judah, saying, Go unto the house of the Rechabites, and speak unto them, and bring them into the house of the LORD, into one of the chambers, and give them wine to drink... And I set before the sons of the house of the Rechabites pots full of wine, and cups, and I said unto them, Drink ye wine. But they said, We will drink no wine: for Jonadab the son of Rechab our father commanded us, saying, Ye shall drink no wine, neither ye, nor your sons forever: Neither shall ye build house, nor sow seed, nor

plant vineyard, nor have any: but all your days ye shall dwell in tents; that ye may live many days in the land where ye be strangers. Thus have we obeyed the voice of Jonadab the son of Rechab our father in all that he hath charged us, to drink no wine all our days, we, our wives, our sons, nor our daughters; The words of Jonadab the son of Rechab, that he commanded his sons not to drink wine, are performed; for unto this day they drink none, but obey their father's commandment: notwithstanding I have spoken unto you, rising early and speaking; but ye hearkened not unto me. (Jeremiah 35:10)

The key to inheriting the blessings, and having the blessings of God manifested in your life is locked into how a person responds to the instructions given. The scripture declares that if you honor your parents you will have a long of life.

Honor thy father and thy mother; that thy days may be long upon the land which the LORD thy God giveth thee. (Exodus 20:12)

For it is written, that Abraham had two sons, the one by a bondmaid, the other by a freewoman. But he who was of the bondwoman was born after the flesh; but he of the freewoman was by promise. (Galatians 4:22, 23)

Abraham had two sons, one he received as the fulfillment of the prophecy, the son of promise. The child was blessed and even followed the footsteps of his father as it was foretold in the scriptures that Abraham would teach his children the ways of the Lord.

On the other hand Abraham's other child was outside God's will.

Wherefore she said unto Abraham, Cast out this bondwoman and her son: for the son of this bondwoman shall not be heir with my son, even with Isaac. (Genesis 21:10)

However, the one that was blessed and followed his father's footstep was the one God gave him as he had promised.

For Sarah conceived, and bare Abraham a son in his old age, at the set time of which God had spoken to him. (Genesis 21:2)

God does not want to condone or sanction our rebellion and our mistakes, but he desires that which is perfect and best for us. Both of them were his sons, but only one had inherited the promises that God had made to Abraham when He said:

And I will make thy seed to multiply as the stars of heaven, and will give unto thy seed all these countries; and in thy seed shall all the nations of the earth be blessed. (Genesis 26:4)

True Sons honor their father's word.

Lo, I come to do thy will, O God. He taketh away the first, that he may establish the second. (Hebrews 10:9)

A closer study on the life of King David's sons will show you that not all his royal children carried themselves worthily. Absalom who is a symbol of rebellion, one of David's sons, did not live up to the expectations of his Father. Rather he gave his father an extraordinary heartache and a really hard time.

And the king said unto Cushi, Is the young man Absalom safe? And Cushi answered, the enemies of my lord the king, and that entire rise against thee to do thee hurt, be as that young man is. And the king was much moved, and went up to the chamber over the gate, and wept: and as he went, thus he said, O my son Absalom, my son, my son Absalom, would God I had died for thee, O Absalom, my son, my son! (2 Samuel 18:33)

Absalom continued to do unspeakable things that did not reflect his father's heart at all. He was consistently a disappointment to his father. But still, he was the son of King David and he bitterly mourned the day of his death because of the sudden end of his life. He mourned because he loved his son, despite his behavior, and because he saw a life, from his own loins for that matter, cut short because of disobedience and rebellion. Absalom had brought about his own death by practicing such things and this caused even deeper sorrow to King David.

Disobedience to parents may lead to premature death, it can breed bitterness in the father's heart, which results in the elimination of one's blessings and inheritance. It is a truthful saying and worthy of all acceptances with scriptural evidence that there are indeed blessings and life bonuses to those children who choose to obey their fathers or parents.

The behavior of Absalom was also evident in the lives of some of David's other sons who didn't follow in their father's footsteps. Unlike Solomon, and in much the same way as Absalom, they were not fit for the throne. In the following chapters we are going to continue to look at some of the outstanding characteristics in Solomon's life that made him unique, and such a quality son that made him therefore a great achiever during his reign - fit for the throne.

DIVINE PROVISION FROM OUTSIDERS

Most of the time, God uses those who are from the household of faith or family, as seen in the case of David and his son, Solomon. Salvation came through God's Son, Jesus

To wit, that God was in Christ, reconciling the world unto himself, not imputing their trespasses unto them; and hath committed unto us the word of reconciliation. (2 Corinthians 5:19)

Solomon responded to the call of stepping into his father's shoes. He had it all figured out, the revelation that this was a partnership between God, his father and himself. With a completely dedicated heart, having counted the cost and having assessed the responsibilities that came with this calling, it was vital that he understood everything exceptionally well. No one can carry out any delegated work without understanding the instructions.

In the case of Solomon, his father's instructions were the key to everything that he was going to do, for his success depended on them. These instructions reflected his father's heart and all that he had in his mind. His rise and fall, his successes and failures, were all summed up in his father's words. This reminds me of a personal example of my son.

One day I came back home from fetching my daughter from school. When I arrived at home my son ran into the driveway to meet me, he was so excited, and at first I did not know what was going on until he started narrating his story. His story went as follows: "I have gone to the next level. I did it daddy, I did it." I asked him what level he was talking about. Then he started reminding me that a few days ago he was trying to get me to help him on his computer game, he was getting stuck on a certain level and he could not proceed to the next level, in this game one graduates upon completing the previous level. In his case he could not because he did not know how to get to the next level. In spite of my attempt to help him I also failed to get him to the next level. It took months since his first attempt for him to break through, but that moment finally came when he came to tell me. I wanted to know how he did it and he told me to come over as he started to demonstrate for me.

It sounded very easy because there was an uncle that was instructing him how to get to the next level. So the key to his next level was the instructions given by this uncle. When he listened and followed the instructions, his final moment of breakthrough manifested.

Allow me to say instruction is the key to the next level, if you want to go to the next level, if you want to go to some place you better find the best instructor you can. Gather up all his information, get the road map, study it thoroughly, make sure you understand it and follow it in detail, and then you will be assured of getting to the place where your dreams will be realized.

KNOWLEDGE: A KEY TO SON-SHIP

One question that a true son (or daughter) should be asking is: What must I do? Or what is expected of me? These questions must be answered properly before any attempt to engage is made. The answers will eliminate all unnecessary hiccups and it will become a pathway to success.

Jesus was able to answer that question and to do what was expected of him by his Father.

Then said I, Lo, I come in the volume of the book it is written of me, to do thy will, O God. (Hebrews 10:7)

Jesus understood his mission and his vision many ages before he was even born. The prophet had already written His job description.

Hence the following Scripture is a testimony of approval of what He came to do from God's perspective. This is what His Father would say:

And a voice from heaven said, "This is My beloved Son, in whom I am well pleased!" (Matthew 3:17)

Doing the will of God pleases God. Nothing breaks God's heart more than a rebellious child.

David mourned for Absalom bitterly when his life ended at an early age. In his example, we see that the consequences of continuous rebellion is to be cut off from inheritances, and more gravely, to have your life cut short.

Jesus said, I came to do my Father's will and to finish it. Everything that He was expected to do was written down. There was a manual written for Him. Jesus said,

It's a volume about me of what I must do and not do. (Hebrews 10:7)

It is the duty of every son to discover and study his assignment. If one does not know his job description he will have serious limitations. Therefore knowledge is power when it goes deeper than mere knowledge; it is about getting a revelation from heaven of your divine assignment.

The key to fulfilling your divine assignment is to access and process the knowledge of what you were created for. Jesus knew why and also where it was written. Go and find your written assignment and what it says about you. Study the details about your assignment and do exactly what it says. God did not give us assignments without giving us a blue print of what He is expecting of us.

Jesus taught in the Lord's Prayer,

Thy will be done in earth, as it is in heaven. (Matthew 6:10)

Often a will is something that is properly written and put down together and it contains legalities of how the estate must be properly distributed. What is written in the will is final and cannot be changed.

CHAPTER 2

THE COST OF SONSHIP

Jesus' life was the ultimate price for the salvation of mankind. His death, burial and resurrection were proof that he paid in full the debt of sin and finally reconciled man to God. For mankind to be saved it required a price. The wages of sin is death and it took the death of Jesus Christ on the cross for us to be bought back into relationship with God.

For ye are bought with a price: therefore glorify God in your body, and in your spirit, which are God's. (1 Corinthians 6:20)

Salvation is by grace through faith in Jesus the Christ. On the cross Jesus cried out to God and said, "Why have you forsaken me?" He was forsaken that we may be accepted. Jesus went through the pain of the cross as a son; he had to go through that process of humiliation, suffering a shameful death, because it was the only way that the world would be saved. He embodied the final sacrifice for the sins mankind.

There is no more price or offering that must be given for our sins. The finished work of the cross has allowed us access into a relationship with God. Jesus in his very own words cried out it is finished. Indeed the price was paid in full.

Often, people want to change the will of God. By so doing they bring upon themselves many sorrows. Don't try and change God's will because your joy depends on it. Your assignment is revealed through your communion with God in your place of prayer.

You must invest quality time in God, in order for you to make it to your destiny. There are no short cuts when it comes to our dealings with God. Consecration paves the way. Jesus said of those who want to be his disciples to "take up your cross daily". This speaks of sacrificing our own desires for His. There are no shortcuts.

For this reason many failed to observe the conditions as they are not always easy. Faithfulness and hard work is the pre-requisite. In the case of Solomon he was not the only one in the family. He did not have the best background. The marriage of his mother and father was scandalous to begin with. His brother Absalom was ruthlessly rebellious, not to mention the other brothers, yet he was heir to the throne. How?

And David sent and enquired after the woman. And one said, Is not this Bathsheba, the daughter of Eliam, the wife of Uriah the Hittite? And David sent messengers, and took her; and she came in unto him, and he lay with her; And the woman conceived, and sent and told David, and said, I am with child. (2 Samuel 11:3 - 5)

And when the mourning was past, David sent and fetched her to his house, and she became his wife, and bare him a son. But the thing that David had done displeased the LORD. (2 Samuel 11:27)

There were characteristics in his life that set him apart for his assignment. There was a stigma attached to Solomon's name, while on the other hand in the royal house there were some hotheaded people, including one of his brothers who was covetous of the same position of becoming the next king. On the very same day Solomon was appointed to be king his brother went ahead to appoint himself to be the next king, without the knowledge and the blessings of his father, David. The royal house had a strong competition going on behind the scenes. This was not merely a strong competition. It was a fight to the death. This was division and dissension, and strife and conflict in every sense of the words!

Solomon's succession to his father's throne demanded him to be tough and strong in order for him to overcome the imposters and great opposition if his throne was to be a success. He had enough support in the sense that his coming to the throne was ordained by God and with his father's full support. After all, it was revealed to his father by God that Solomon was to be his successor. His name appeared in the journals of his father David that he was indeed his father's choice.

Allow me to say there was a prophetic word that confirmed his appointment. If God is on your side you can withstand any opposition. If God be for you who can be against you?

What shall we then say to these things? If God be for us, who can be against us? (Romans 8:31)

It was more than the will of his father; it was the will of God which qualified him to be the right candidate for the job. Among the people that stood side by side with him were the Priests and the Prophets, or one would say a godly accompaniment, the very mouthpieces of God. With this support base it made it easier for him to overcome the domestic opposition that was vicious even in the natural.

The restructuring and the pulling down of strongholds that were rooted within the family was one of his greatest assignments. Jesus said "a prophet has no honor in his own town", and they were offended in him.

But Jesus said unto them, "A prophet is not without honor, save in his own country, and in his own house." (Matt 13:57)

Jesus' greatest opposition was among His own people and that led to His ultimate death on the cross. The worst enemies one can have are those of his own household.

Similarly Abraham's life can give us some lessons regarding family matters as he had to make tough decisions on the issues regarding his nephew when they had to resolve a dispute that was among them that resulted in them parting ways.

And there was strife between the herdsmen of Abram's cattle and the herdsmen of Lot's cattle: and the Canaanite and the Perizzite dwelled then in the land. Then Lot chose him all the plain of Jordan; and Lot journeyed east: and they separated themselves the one from the other. (Genesis 13:7, 11)

In order to fulfill your assignment sometimes you have to let go of those who are close to you even though it's a high price to pay. It's not easy to let go of your loved ones, but if that is what it takes to get the work done there is no other way but to let them go.

And every one that hath forsaken houses, or brethren, or sisters, or father, or mother, or wife, or children, or lands, for my name's sake, shall receive a hundredfold, and shall inherit everlasting life. (Matthew 19:29)

In Solomon's case he had to learn the hard way as he had to get rid one of his brothers to find a way to overcome the adversity his brother was bringing even though it meant killing him. He had to be tough or else lose his job and consequently, his kingdom.

Jesus said my assignment is to do God's will. The sum total of sonship is to do. There is a story in the Bible of two sons who were sent to do a task, one said I won't do it and the other said I will do it.

But what think ye? A certain man had two sons; and he came to the first, and said, Son, go work today in my vineyard. He answered and said, I will not: but afterward he repented, and went. And he came to the second, and said likewise. And he answered and said, I go, sir: and went not. (Matthew 21:28 —30)

The one who said I won't do it ended up doing and the one who said I will do, did not do. It's not in your word but

in your actions, it's not your lip service but your actions that determines your actual service. It's not what you say but what you do. Be a doer of the word not a hearer only. But be ye doers of the word, and not hearers only, deceiving your own selves. (James 1:22)

Many have heard but few have done. Which category are you in? Are you in the hearing category or in the doing category? Do you do what you have heard? If you are not doing what you have heard you are not paying the price of your assignment. Getting rid of bad company is part of the game plan.

Solomon came into a kingdom that was not perfect, where there was a lot of cleaning to be done. Even his father told him there was a need to get rid of some bad apples, in case they may end up spoiling the bunch. His father told him that he was a wise man and that he knew what to do. In other words he was encouraging him to use his God given wisdom on what to do to fulfill his role in that particular matter.

Wisdom is essential in leadership. One must observe, listen carefully, and implement the principles. He had to clean out all corrupt elements that would side track his progress. He did not allow hypocrites, double-minded, and unlawful people to work alongside him. He was not going to be successful if he was going to compromise or try to please his fellow men. The only thing he had to do was to employ high standards of administration and most importantly, seek to please God rather than man.

Solomon did not get caught up in the same corruption as his brothers due to the fact that he was familiar with their activities and on his part he knew his job description and his assignment.

It is absolutely essential to study your assignment and know your way around it. Get a full description of your vision and know exactly what God says to you.

God spoke to David and said, "Your son will be the one to build me a house" and David handed over that responsibility to his son Solomon as God ordered him. David told Solomon, 'At first I thought it was me who was supposed to do this job but now it is your assignment'. Solomon carried out this work with the full understanding that this was a vision from his father and that God had recommended that he be the one to carry it out. Just find the original manuscript of the vision, handle it with dedication and you will be good to go. Solomon took heed to what he was instructed by his father.

I want us to take a close study of his speech and the motive behind it. On the day of the inauguration of the Temple he gave a speech that was not full of self praises, boasting, or self-elevation; neither did he credit himself for his accomplishment. His speech was simple and full of humility, pointing out that all that he had done was not of his own volition. If it was not his idea whose idea was it? The following passage provides the answer as he addressed thousands of people who had gathered to witness this historic moment.

Solomon stood upon this vast and magnificent architectural work that had never been seen before under the sun and gave one of the most humble of speeches ever heard. We can only imagine what was going through his mind; I think he wished his father was present to witness the answer to his prayers and the fulfillment of the Word of the Lord. Hence his opening words were to honor his Father:

And it was in the heart of David my father to build a house for the name of the LORD God of Israel. (I Kings 8:17)

As we continue with this study we will find out that which was in the heart of David when he said he wanted to build a house for God. What kind of a house did David have in mind? We are going to look at a number of things that were in the Temple that Solomon built which he got from the original plan of David.

HIS BUILDING

One of Solomon's earliest building projects was to construct the Temple, which David had dreamed of building. Hiram, King of Tyre, provided cedar trees from Mount Lebanon for the Temple and he was repaid in food (1 Kings 5:1-2). To provide workers for these building projects, the Canaanites were made slaves (1 Kings 9:20-21). Israelites likewise were forced to work in groups of 10,000 (1 Kings 5:13-18, 2 Chronicles 2:17-18). The workers for the Temple alone included 80,000 stonecutters, 70,000 common laborers and 3,600 foremen.

He built a structure that was to be used for multi-cultural purposes and he used people of different cultures to produce the vision. To accomplish great things in life you need to involve people of all walks of life.

The church in Jerusalem did not grow as fast as the one in Antioch because they did not involve everyone. In the case of Solomon, he brought everyone to the table. I would call this The United Nations Building.

It took seven years to finish the Temple, which by modern standards was a rather small edifice; 90 feet (27.4 meters) long, 30 feet (9.1 meters) wide and 45 feet (13.7 meters) high. The gold covering put over the walls and furniture made it exquisite.

In the eleventh year of Solomon's reign, the dedication of the Temple was celebrated (1 Kings 6:38, 1 Kings 8:1-5). The Presence of the Lord filled the Temple; Solomon then offered a great prayer dedicating the Temple (1 Kings 8:23-53). Afterwards, he offered up 22,000 oxen and 120,000 sheep as well as other offerings. The people were full of joy because such a great king had replaced David.

Just by looking at the number of years it took to complete the Temple I am reminded of the number seven, which speaks of completion and rest. God created the world in six days and rested on the seventh day. It also speaks of covenant blessings as symbolized by the number of colors of the rainbow. The rainbow symbolizes the covenant that God made after the flood during Noah's time that He will not destroy the world with a flood ever again.

And the rainbow shall be in the cloud. And I will look upon it that I may remember the everlasting covenant between God and every living creature of all flesh that is upon the earth. (Genesis 9:18)

The rainbow also speaks of beauty. Speaking of beauty, this project was possibly the most beautiful building ever built at that time. It was the talk of the day and people came from near and far to witness this great achievement. It was indeed one of the most beautiful and glorious buildings that everyone, everywhere was speaking about and it became a national monument.

Solomon built other buildings also:

The house of the Forest of Lebanon, the Hall of Pillars, a hall of his throne, and a house for the daughter of Pharaoh. (I Kings 7:2-8)

Thirteen years were involved in a building of his own house, which was large enough to take care of his many wives, concubines and servants. A great fortress, Malo, was also built, which was used to protect the Temple. (I Kings 9:24)

The Temple was just the beginning of his many great achievements. It seems like if someone begins right and does the first things first, everything else just falls in place.

There are no shortcuts to spiritual son-ship

I would like to share some of my own experiences I've had with my spiritual sons. Some were good and some were really challenging. When I travel to different countries, I meet people of different nationalities. Some of these people seem to be genuinely drawn to me. Others are not genuine. I have become so familiar with words such as, "Will you please father me in the faith?" These words come from married couples, pastors and individuals of all ages asking will you please father us? In the past I was not sure what to say or how to respond. Now with wisdom and experience, I have learned to properly discern who is coming in the right spirit and who is not.

I've come to notice that there are people out there who "shop" for spiritual fathers just as people go shopping for clothes. In Malachi the Bible says that God is going to turn the hearts of the fathers and sons.

Behold, I will send you Elijah the prophet before the coming of the great and dreadful day of the LORD: And he shall turn the heart of the fathers to the children, and the heart of the children to their fathers, lest I come and smite the earth with a curse. (Malachi 4:5-6)

The truth of the matter is that a father and son relationship must be a turning of the heart by God for both parties. It is a joining of the heart that is divinely orchestrated by God. It is a relationship that is sincere and divinely ordered by God.

I once agreed to father someone in the past without counting the cost. The events that followed that relationship were very bitter. Through God's intervention the relationship was spared and I took it that God was teaching me a valuable lesson through this experience. Allow me to say every relationship goes through a test. People must figure out first why they are going into a relationship otherwise their joy will be short lived.

I now have a way of helping people who come to me for spiritual covering. This is what I tell them: I offer them an opportunity to study me first before I can say anything to them. In most cases I have found out that those that are real will continue to relate with me and those that are not just vanish away.

I remember some place where somebody came after a week and

said, "I can't be your son any more". Then I said, "Yes that's what I'm talking about." People want cheap grace and the moment you start telling them the truth they can't stand it. If you can't be corrected, if you can't submit, if you are not willing to listen then you are stubborn, arrogant and rebellious, and you will not be able to walk in the father and son relationship of which I speak.

Some even think they can buy son-ship. Not so. Son-ship is not a franchise that you pay for annually. There is no price tag to this kind of relationship, as I always say that you can't bribe your way into son-ship. There are no short-cuts to this relationship it must be something legitimate that is directed by God. There are a lot of illegitimate sons who switch camps because they don't want to live up to responsibility and accountability. Yes, I do believe that there are sons that are born in one house and raised in another. God will allow a spiritual adoption. However there must be proper closure at every juncture. There are no short cuts into son-ship.

HIS GOVERNMENT

David had brought the twelve tribes of Israel together, but Solomon organized the entire state with the help of many officials.

So King Solomon was king over all Israel. (1 Kings 4:1)

The entire country was divided into twelve major districts; each district had to pay for the expenses of the King's court for one month each year. The system was fair and distributed the tax burden equally over the entire country. Solomon took everything to the next level - the way he had grasped the vision was like a double portion anointing was upon his life.

Solomon was a man of great grace and he had the ability to organize and delegate officials from every district and every country. He put into place financial administrators for the distribution of taxes throughout the country thereby bringing peace even as his name entails. Throughout his reign there was much peace everywhere. He was indeed a man who was flowing in the blessings of his father.

There is great reward in walking in your father's vision. Indeed his government was the most powerful government that ever existed. His father chose the right man to be the head of state and one would say all went well. Anyone in God's creation will have excellent results if he positions himself correctly - according to his office - and follows his instructions to the end.

In the first year of his reign I Daniel understood by books the number of the years, whereof the word of the LORD came to Jeremiah the prophet, that he would accomplish seventy years in the desolations of Jerusalem. (Daniel 9:2)

Just as Daniel had done, Solomon too did everything by the book. He did not add or take anything out from what his father had put into his hands. Just like Daniel, he worked on the blueprint as a faithful steward and by so doing he completed his task. The whole world came to him to copy his style of government. His leadership style was admired by all who came across him: Just like Daniel when he understood everything by the book, what God had said through the prophet Jeremiah. Being a student of the word, he understood what he learnt, he obtained wisdom and understanding from them and began to draw some strategies that in turn gave him favor and honor. People must take everything from what the word of God says if they are to live and enjoy the full blessings of God in this world and the hereafter. Solomon did not leave any stone unturned. Putting into practice all that he was told by his father was the secret to his success. Doing everything by the book to the last word was what made him the greatest leader of all time.

Kingdom Business

The kings had an agreement with Hiram, king of Tyre. For cedar trees, stonecutters and other buildings, Solomon paid 125,000 bushels (4,4 million liters) of wheat and 115,000 gallons (435,275 liters) of olive oil every year.

And Solomon gave Hiram twenty thousand measures of wheat for food to his household, and twenty measures of pure oil: thus gave Solomon to Hiram year by year. (1 Kings 5:11)

In addition, Hiram received twenty cities in Galilee to cover all indebtedness. Although Israel's law forbade the trading of horses,

But he shall not multiply horses to himself, nor cause the people to return to Egypt, to the end that he should multiply horses: forasmuch as the LORD hath said unto you, Ye shall henceforth return no more that way. (Deuteronomy 17:16)

Solomon bought horses and chariots from the Egyptians and some of these in turn were sold to the Hittites and Arameans at a profit (1 Kings 10:28-29).

Furthermore, Solomon engaged in sea trade. Ships built in shipyards at Ezion-geber sailed to parts of the Red sea and Indian Ocean. The sailors collected gold, ivory and peacocks. From Ophir, the traders brought back 420 talents of gold, a considerable fortune.

Solomon was a successful business man who made profit in all major currencies; nations brought riches to him. Blessings overflowed. When one is blessed he is not limited geographically. The blessings have the tendency to transform one's background. The world came to him and did not come empty handed. Kings from near and far, Africa included, came to behold the glory of the one that was excelling because he chose to honor the vision of his father and to build according to the instructions of his father.

THE WISEST MAN THAT EVER LIVED

This is a list of some of Solomon's achievements:

- He was strong in many gifts and colorful as a rainbow.
- A powerful author: The book of Proverbs, Song of Solomon

and Ecclesiastes in the Bible are part of his inspired work. He was indeed a king, powerful inspired best-selling author, and a successful businessman.

- Solomon wrote 3,000 proverbs and over 1,000 songs (1 Kings 4:32). Most of the book of proverbs is attributed to him (Proverbs 22:1) as well as Ecclesiastes, Song of Songs, Psalms 72 and 127. The Bible particularly mentions his accomplishment as a writer. (1Kings 11:41)

- The Queen of Sheba came from Africa to see and hear if the reports of Solomon's fame and wisdom were true. After viewing all he had in Jerusalem and hearing his wisdom, she blessed the Lord God of Israel for raising such a wise person to sit upon such a magnificent throne. (1 Kings 10:1)

SOLOMON'S MANPOWER

Moreover there are workmen with thee in abundance, hewers and workers of stone and timber, and all manner of cunning men for every manner of work. Of the gold, the silver, and the brass, and the iron, there is no number. Arise herefore, and be doing, and the LORD be with thee. (1 Chronicles 22:15 —16)

It is quite interesting to note that in doing God's work it is good to work with those God brings to the work. Solomon's manpower was provided by his father. The short-listing and the hiring of the laborers was done by his father - the draftsmen, the designers, bricklayers... they were all provided to carry out what was in his father's heart. They were recruited from the nation of Israel and from foreign countries. He had international building constructors.

In the same way when Jesus began His ministry He did not hire without consulting God. He prayed to His Father all night before hiring. The best workmen come from God.

And it came to pass in those days, that he went out into a mountain to pray, and continued all night in prayer to God. And when it was day, he called unto him his disciples: and of them he chose twelve, whom also he named apostles; (Luke 6:12, 13)

To have a team that will build and finish, you need the divine selection of God. Nehemiah refused to work with anyone that had a wrong motive. There is a great need to work with those that understand the vision and have the right motive. Henry Ford said: "I will build a car for the great multitude. It will be large enough for the family, but small enough for the individual to run and care for, it will be constructed of the best materials by the best men to be hired, after the simplest design that modern engineering can devise; but it will be so low in price that no man making a good salary will be unable to own one, and enjoy with his family the blessings of hours of pleasure in God's great open spaces". He had a vision to build a car using the best men available, as laborers.

Both Solomon and Jesus were to implement their fathers' vision as per their fathers' plan without changing it one bit.

DON'T SEEK FOR RECOGNITION, RECOGNITION WILL SEEK FOR YOU

When Solomon's fame went throughout the whole world one would say it was because of his singleness of purpose and pure motives. When a person has a clean and clear intention, the entirety of his work will be all right. His goal was to achieve what God assigned to his father, building as he was instructed, and reigning to the glory of God. He was seeking first the kingdom of God and His righteousness and when he did that all things were added to him.

Let me use some of his own words from some passages of the books he wrote he said:

A good name is better than precious ointment; and the

day of death than the day of one's birth." (Ecc. 7:1) "A good name is rather to be chosen than great riches, and loving favor rather than silver and gold. (Proverbs 22:1)

A good name will advertise itself. It was not long even before people from Africa heard about Solomon. Queen of Sheba had come all the way from Ethiopia in Africa to come and see this great king.

And when the queen of Sheba heard of the fame of Solomon concerning the name of the LORD, she came to prove him with hard questions. (1 Kings 10:1)

There are many people today who want the whole world to hear about them and they do all they can to be heard. They advertise themselves and put their names on the World Wide Web. It's not about what you do to be heard it's about what God can do through you. What God has done through you is the only cause that can bring the whole world to you and get you connected. Your testimony supersedes your advertisement. Like Jesus, your testimony needs to go before you. He did not bribe the media or give tips and incentives to anyone to promote himself. The gift of God in you will make you famous.

A man's gift makes room for him and brings him before great men. (Proverbs 8:16)

When you are enthroned by commission, not by omission, you will not go to the world, but the world will come to you. The gift of God will gather people around you; Solomon's wisdom went beyond him and gave him an audience.

A good name is better than precious ointment; and the day of death than the day of one's birth. (Ecclesiastes 7:1)

A good name is better than precious oil; this is another quote from one of his publications.

CHAPTER 3

THE TESTIMONY

Solomon's kingship made some worldwide headlines. People from distant countries and neighboring countries became interested in his style of ruling. One would say he was his father's choice, and graced by God's wisdom and honor. There was no one like him during or after his life time.. He was a well decorated king. His testimony superseded his name. Indeed his success became a good representation of his father's name. He was a true statesman whose achievement and success received worldwide recognition. The whole global community was focused on his kingdom and his success. His tremendous achievements became the primary marketing tool for his country and consequently brought about a great turnover in foreign currency. His policies attracted foreign investors who in turn brought in their products; imported goods, spices and oil were among the list that came into Jerusalem.

It is important to note that in his entire success story Solomon did not overlook who was behind it. Hence these following golden words that he spoke in recognition to that fact, I quote, "It was in my father's heart to build a house for God". In other words he was saying "once upon a time there was a man who had dreamed to build this house." He was simply saying, "I'm not the great boy you think I am, you may call me great but I am not ignorant of my hero. I am not that powerful, there is no way I might have completed this house without the man whom you should actually give all the credit, and that man is my father. He was my main inspiration, my coach and my financier as well as my business partner. He is the one that put together this building plan and all the necessary things that enabled me to do what I did. This magnificent piece of work that you see is his entire idea."

There is nothing that can be compared with the power of agreement.

When people come into partnership and allow themselves to work as a team, things begin to happen. Even the word of God has something to say about that.

If two of you shall agree on earth as touching anything that they shall ask, it shall be done for them of my Father which is in heaven. (Matthew 18:19)

In the case of Solomon one can concede that there was an agreement between him and his father. His words said it all; his speech indicated a real partnership. Covenant was the key to his testimony. He started with his father and it was not long before the news reached the whole world. This news spread like wild fire.

There is a classic story in the Bible that gives us a picture concerning teamwork. It is a story of a group of people who came together to build. Their building began to progress because their partnership was so strong and so real. It actually took God and the angels to stop them from carrying on. These people were united, they had one language and they succeeded in whatever they wanted to do.

And they said one to another, Go to, let us make bricks, and burn them thoroughly. And they had brick for stone, and slime had they for mortar. And they said, Go to, let us build us a city and a tower, whose top may reach unto heaven; and let us make us a name, lest we be scattered abroad upon the face of the whole earth. And the LORD came down to see the city and the tower, which the children of men built. And the LORD said, Behold, the people is one, and they have all one language; and this they begin to do: and now nothing will be restrained from them, which they have imagined to do. Go to, let us go down, and there confound their language, that they may not understand one another's speech. So the LORD scattered them abroad from thence upon the face of all the earth: and they left off to build the city. (Genesis 11:3-8)

This story seeks to address the power of partnership. Even when God came to inspect what they were building he confirmed that these people were capable of completing what they had begun, because they were one. In the case of Solomon, he was not just trying to put a building together - he was working together with God. God working through Solomon's life attracted most of the world leaders to come and seek advice and guidance from Solomon. God had blessed him with godly wisdom; his counsel to other kings was well sought after.

Solomon was a believer who was in covenant with God. He operated and functioned through words of knowledge and wisdom. In the New Testament this is known as the gifts of the spirit.

For to one is given by the Spirit the word of wisdom; to another the word of knowledge by the same Spirit; (1 Corinthians 12:8)

Solomon's father David echoed this principle when he said,

The fear of the LORD is the beginning of wisdom: a good understanding have all they that do his commandments: his praise endureth forever. (Psalm 111:10)

The church of the Living God has received a vision; this vision has been made clear with all the details of how it must be implemented. The Commander in Chief, the Lord Jesus Christ, specified that world evangelism must begin in Jerusalem (Acts 1:8) and move to the other regions thereafter, and ultimately to the uttermost parts of the world. The New Testament church was in agreement with heaven. They were representing the will of God on earth, just as it is in heaven. It was in a very short period of time that their testimony reached the whole world, from Jerusalem to the uttermost parts of the world. They became one of the most powerful organizations on the earth; allow me to call them the unstoppable. The authorities of their time accused them of turning the world upside down. Their influence affected both sectors of society. The wealthy came with their support while the poor came to receive ministry and have their basic needs met. Their infrastructure, model of ministry, and their message cannot be compared with what we have in our modern world. They had no cars, no radios, no televisions, yet they preached out loud and 3,000 people were converted in a single meeting.

Then they that gladly received his word were baptized: and the same day there were added unto them about three thousand souls. (Act 2:41)

Another 5,000 were converted thereafter. The reason they had such a great number of followers was because of their testimony. When God sends people with a message, people will respond and give their support. One of the signs that confirm the Word of God is the provision of resources that accompanies it. In the case of Solomon the whole world came to join him including Queen of Sheba who came all the way from Africa with her Ethiopian spices and jewelry.

The New Testament Church had a powerful testimony: they had a divine capability and a unique characteristic that influenced the whole world. What we need is a testimony that speaks of God in us.

CHAPTER 4

WORLDWIDE RECOGNITION

Solomon's gifts and calling were not limited by location. He oversaw the construction of the Temple, whose architectural features and beauty were world class. We have heard about the Seven Wonders of the World. These seven wonders have made an impact on the world at large. Their beauty is praised of throughout the world.

The wisdom of Solomon was undoubtedly unique and unprecedented. This wisdom is particularly highlighted in the following story:

Then spake the woman whose living child was unto the king, for her bowels yearned upon her son, and she said, O my lord, give her the living child, and in no wise slay it. But the other said, Let it be neither mine nor thine, but divide it. Then the king answered and said, Give her the living child, and in no wise slay it: she is the mother thereof. And all Israel heard of the judgment which the king had judged; and they feared the king: for they saw that the wisdom of God was in him, to do judgment. (1 Kings 3:26-28)

The approach Solomon used in this case was so outstanding that the news made worldwide headlines.

Wisdom, like the other spiritual gifts is universal; they are not limited by region or any geographical boundaries. There is neither speech nor language that can function as a hindrance to understanding these gifts. One of the most unique things about the construction of Solomon's building was the inclusion of different nationalities working on it.

The exclusive, imported material that at the end gave the building a universal and an international status was something the whole world could identify with it.

On the day he dedicated the Temple he made it clear in his prayers that he wanted all the nations to be part of the community worship center and to be blessed. Would it be possible that he did not want to overlook their input and assistance during the construction which had such an impact on the outcome of this project that he felt it was proper for him to acknowledge and welcome them as his global prayer partners? His desire was that in the future they may come to worship, participate and benefit from the blessings that were encompassed in this wonderful and beautiful Temple.

Consequently when finished, the building had worldwide recognition, more so because in his Temple he welcomed all races and all nations; there was no segregation whatsoever. It is stated in the scriptures that God said to Adam:

Be fruitful, and multiply, and replenish the earth, and subdue it: and have dominion over the fish of the sea, and over the fowl of the air, and over every living thing that moveth upon the earth. (Genesis 1:28)

The word *"subduing"* implies conquest or vanquishing. God wants all His people to be fruitful and to subdue the earth. The fruit of your labor must be seen in the earth, for this is God's intention for humankind.

As I said earlier, subduing implies conquest or vanquishing. In other words subdue denotes the fact of "transcending", which means "to have influence beyond, over and above, your region or your locality". As the word of God declares,

Ye have not chosen me, but I have chosen you, and ordained you, that ye should go and bring forth fruit, and that your fruit should remain: that whatsoever ye shall ask of the Father in my name, he may give it you. (John 15:16)

You were created to be influential beyond where you live. Someone somewhere can benefit from what you have. It is about time that you realize that you were created for the world, and not just your nation. Your physical presence does not matter; you can still reach beyond where you are without physically getting there.

Your gift, therefore, must transcend cultural barriers that you may become part of a global blessing in a global community. The Bible says:

We are seated with Christ Jesus in the heavenly places far above principalities and powers, which He wrought in Christ, when He raised Him from the dead, and set Him at his own right hand in the heavenly places, Far above all principality, and power, and might, and dominion, and every name that is named, not only in this world, but also in that which is to come. (Ephesians 1:20-21)

Our position is both spiritual and physical - we are in the world but we are not of this world. When the Bible says we are seated with Christ in heavenly places, that's not a geographical position but a spiritual one, where we begin to influence things in the spiritual realm. With our prayers we can reach the whole world. Your prayers can save a child in war-troubled Somalia; they can reach somebody in the gulf region of Iraq or Iran. Hence Solomon's prayer was a universal prayer, everyone was included. He prayed a holistic prayer, a prayer for the whole world. One would say he was building an international house of prayer, a universal building and a house of prayer for all nations.

Jesus gave a great commission in the book of Mathew.

Go ye therefore, and teach all nations, baptizing them in the name of the Father, and of the Son, and of the Holy Ghost: (Mathew 28:19)

And the whole world belongs to God; He has the whole world in His hand. We are the people who represent the kingdom of God and the whole world must know about it and we carry a message of hope, grace, mercy, and the deliverance of God.

CHAPTER 5

THE GLORY AND JOY

Now when Solomon had made an end of praying, the fire came down from heaven, and consumed the burnt offering and the sacrifices; and the glory of the LORD filled the house. (2 Chronicles 7:1)

This scripture documents what happened after Solomon's prayer. The glory of the Lord filled the Temple. Seemingly, Solomon did not "miss" what he had learnt from his father. He brought into reality what his father intended from the onset. He represented his father's vision in a worthy manner. He was indeed in agreement with his father's vision. His prayer was nothing else but the plea of his father. He was earnestly telling God what he heard from his father. He reminded God of His father's intentions, and sought God to come and do a divine inspection in hopes of the Almighty putting His seal of approval upon the completion of his work.

It looks like God was pleased with his humble and unselfish prayer. Solomon was simply saying, "I was obedient, I have done what my father told me to do; he told me to build a house for your name because you told him that I was the man to do it." When he was saying this, God came and validated this work. And the above mentioned scripture says it all.

God answered him in a dramatic way. There were few incidents in the Bible where God answered in such a way, after man had prayed.

There was an incident on Mount Sinai where God appeared in such a visible way after Moses prayed. The kind of prayers that brings the glory of God in such a unique and tangible way are those that are prayed In agreement with God. I call them prayers of glory where the heavens agree with someone on earth as the Scripture declares:

And I will give unto thee the keys of the kingdom of heaven: and whatsoever thou shalt bind on earth shall be bound in heaven: and whatsoever thou shall loose on earth shall be loosed in heaven; (Matthew 16:19)

Let us pray! It's about time for God to come and appear in a glorious way. We need to be praying prayers that move heaven, declaring and reminding God of what is in His Word. Smith Wigglesworth, known as the "Apostle of faith", once said, "Prayer is simply reminding God of what is in His Word". When these types of prayers are prayed, then we will see the glory of God as Solomon and his people did. When God can confirm Himself it will serve as an agreement that God is indeed with us. Elijah prayed to God and fire came down. It was one way of God saying "yes" to Elijah, "I am in agreement with your prayers. I am the real God the God of your forefathers."

Let us revisit the prayer of Elijah as he challenged the prophets of Baal.

And you call on the name of your gods, and I will call on the name of Jehovah. And it shall be, the god that answers by fire, He is God. And all the people answered and said, the word is good. (1Kings 18:24)

This scripture shows a classic demonstration of God's visible presence after prayer.

Solomon's prayer released an overwhelming joy to all the people of God. The following scripture speaks of the face of God shinning on the people and releasing joy.

God be merciful unto us, and bless us; and cause his face to shine upon us. (Psalm 67:1)

Wilt thou not revive us again: that thy people may rejoice in thee? (Psalm 85:6)

44

There are so many people who gather today in the name of God, and yet His presence is not there. They do not experience the joy of the Lord because the presence of the Lord is not in their midst, and the Lord will not be part of the gathering.

Solomon's Temple was filled with the glory of God which was visible beyond doubt. When we build our lives upon God's word the glory of God will be our portion.

Jesus prayed and said, "and now, O Father, glorify thou me with thine own self with the glory which I had with thee before the world was... and the glory which thou gavest me I have given them; that they may be one, even as we are one." (John 17:5, 22)

The reason why the glory of God is so scarce is because of sin. Sin speaks of missing the mark, and when people have missed the mark just as Adam did, the world inherited sin.

For all have sinned, and come short of the glory of God. (Romans 3:23)

God's original intention was that we may have His glory. Jesus came to restore us back into our original state. He brought the glory of God, the grace of God and the truth (John 1:14). He called us, justified us and He also glorified us.

Moreover whom he did predestinate, them he also called: and whom he called, them he also justified: and whom he justified, them he also glorified. (Romans 8:30)

Solomon's Temple was a visible picture of the type of glory that was to come.

The glory of this latter house shall be greater than of the former, saith the LORD of hosts: and in this place will I give peace, saith the LORD of hosts. (Haggai 2:9)

The Church of Jesus Christ is the church that will have the glory of God just as Jesus prayed that the glory be given to the Church; we are the Temple of the Holy Ghost:

Do you not know that your body is a temple of the Holy Spirit who is in you, whom you have received from God? You are not your own. (2 Corinthians 6:19)

The question may be asked, if the physical Temple of Solomon under the Old Testament order was filled with glory of God, how much more the church of Jesus Christ under the new covenant, which is based upon better promises? Paul said,

To whom God would make known what is the riches of the glory of this mystery among the Gentiles; which is Christ in you, the hope of glory. (Colossians 1:27)

All who serve God in Christ have been brought into a covenant relationship which allows them to be partakers of the glory of God. The word "glory" means every component that makes God to be God. When the glory of God is in our lives we will be able to function as sons of God by doing as Jesus did, gracefully and truthfully. Paul declares,

I am crucified with Christ: nevertheless I live; yet not I, but Christ liveth in me: and the life which I now live in the flesh I live by the faith of the Son of God, who loved me, and gave himself for me. (Galatians 2:20)

God looks forward to the generation that is coming, one that will operate and function just like Jesus. The days of playing church politics, using religious gimmicks and competitions, are coming to an end. God is raising a church that will respect, and honor each other in the fear of God. Allow me to suggest that the reason why the glory of God came upon Solomon's work was because he had a pure motive. He was motivated by the vision that came from his father, even as it can be seen in his own words:

And it was in the heart of David my father to build a house for the name of Jehovah, the God of Israel. (2 Chronicles 6:7)

Whose vision are we trying to complete, our own vision or God's vision? Who are we imitating, the Son of God or our own fellow men? Jesus said,

And I say also unto thee, That thou art Peter, and upon this rock I will build my church; and the gates of hell shall not prevail against it. (Matthew 16:18)

It is His church that He is building through us for Himself. It is His kingdom,

For thine is the Kingdom, and the power, and the glory, forever. Amen. (Matthew 6:13)

It's through His glory by His grace. Let us all acknowledge this and be able to say it is God's vision that the whole world be filled with His glory for His honor. God is looking for glorious people not a glory-less people. Jeremiah once asked this question,

How is the gold become dim! How is the finest gold changed! the stones of the sanctuary are poured out in the top of every street? (Lamentations 4:1)

In other words he was saying the people who are supposed to glow with the glory of God have become dull. Why is the church that is supposed to walk in the supernatural power of God becoming powerless? Why is the church that is supposed to be glorious glory-less? If you compare the scriptures regarding the times that we are living in, and what the church should be like, you may come to the conclusion that the church is in a state of backsliding. Could it be possible that those that are building today are not building for Him but for themselves? What would have happened If Solomon had decided to slightly alter the plans that his father had given him? Would he have achieved the same result? Would it have changed the whole picture? Would he have seen the glory in the Temple? Would he have experienced the joy that he experienced?

CHAPTER 6

THE FATHER'S HEARTBEAT

GOD'S HEARTBEAT THROUGH WORSHIP

Jesus revealed one the most profound principles of the kingdom of heaven: the principle of true worship. The woman who he spoke to at the well of Samaria had a misconception about worship, where to worship and how to worship. However Jesus gave her a class on the subject as we can see In the following passage.

But the hour cometh, and now is, when the true worshippers shall worship the Father in spirit and in truth: for the Father seeketh such to worship him. God is a Spirit: and they that worship him must worship him in spirit and in truth. (John 4:23)

Jesus was referring to the heartbeat of God, indicating that true worshipers are those that worship God in spirit and in truth. Similarly David was a man with a passion for worship and God calls him a man after His own heart. Heaven is all about worship. The dwelling place of God is all about worship. That is the only activity that takes place around the throne of God continuously. David's passion was for the presence and his son, Solomon, tapped into the same dimension of the grace of the presence and worship just like his father. It is interesting to note that Solomon grew up to become like his father. The house that he was building which was his father's vision was for one purpose - which was the worship of God. Isaiah puts it this way: "I and the sons God has given me are for signs and wonders". Solomon had his father's heartbeat. He stopped at nothing until he had fulfilled that which was in his father's heart, to establish a house that will entail the presence of God. David's priority when he became the king was to bring the Ark of the Covenant to Jerusalem. The Ark of the Covenant represents the glory of God or the presence of God. David wanted to make sure that the God's presence dwelled where he was seated as king, and he therefore did everything in his power to bring the Ark of the Covenant into his kingdom. Similarly, Solomon is seen tapping into the same grace which was confirmed on the day of the dedication of the temple, when the glory of God came and filled the temple. David's deepest desire and passion as mentioned above was for the presence of God. He had the zeal to chase after God's own heart as seen in the scripture below.

As the hart panteth after the water brooks, so panteth my soul after thee, O God. My soul thirsteth for God, for the living God: when shall I come and appear before God? (Psalm 42:1-2)

GOD'S HEARTBEAT IS FOUND THROUGH REPENTANCE

Man in his own cannot save himself. God sent His Son to come to seek that which was lost. God does not delight in the death of a sinner. Therefore His heartbeat is to see man reconciled back to God. This can only be done through God himself reaching out to the sinner. God is a soul winner at heart. That is supported by the evidence that we find in the book of Genesis.

And the LORD God called unto Adam, and said unto him, where art thou? (Genesis 3:9)

God sought to restore him. It is the same today. God seeks for his lost creation, as the Bible declares,

Come now, and let us reason together, saith the LORD: though your sins be as scarlet, they shall be as white as snow; though they be red like crimson, they shall be as wool. (Isaiah 1:18)

Here, Isaiah pounds the importance of reasoning. As God calls mankind, His appeal to us is to see sense in everything we do. God did not abandon Adam because of the mistakes he did, but rather offered him a second chance. He is a loving God and longsuffering, who is consistently reaching out for the lost soul. Allow me to say He is the ultimate soul winner.

For the Son of man is come to seek and to save that which was lost. (Luke 19:10)

The son of God came to seek and save the lost. You have to love what your father loves and hate what your father hates. Jesus had a zeal for the father's house; He remembered that it was written,

The zeal of thine house hath eaten me up. (John 2:17)

Jesus deepest desire was to see people saved and delivered from sin and the power of the devil. More than that, He wanted to see people worshiping God in Spirit and in truth. He dealt thoroughly with those who abused the Temple, the place of worship, by driving them away from it - reminding them that the house of God was not meant for merchandising.

And said unto them, It is written, My house shall be called the house of prayer; but ye have made it a den of thieves. (Matthew 21:13)

He told them about the purpose of the house of His father and He did not compromise like the priest who had charge over the Temple. He took the situation into His own hands. He was very personal about it. Anyone abusing his father's house was not acceptable; One would say He took personal ownership of His father's property.

Solomon had a similar zeal when he built a house of prayer for all nations. Solomon's name means peace. Similarly, Jesus is the prince of peace. They indeed shared a common vision of honoring their fathers' vision. Jesus' first sermon was in the house of God.

And he came to Nazareth, where he had been brought

up: and, as his custom was, he went into the synagogue on the sabbath day, and stood up for to read. And there was delivered unto him the book of the prophet Isaiah. And when he had opened the book, he found the place where it was written, The Spirit of the Lord is upon me, because he hath anointed me to preach the gospel to the poor; he hath sent me to heal the brokenhearted, to preach deliverance to the captives, and recovering of sight to the blind, to set at liberty them that are bruised, (Luke 4:16-18)

According to Jesus' order of priorities God's work must be first.

Everything begins with God. Without God there is no beginning. Everything in life must find its origin in God.

In the beginning God created the heaven and the earth. (Genesis 1:1)

Solomon's top priority was to build the house of God first, and then his house, and everything else thereafter. On the contrary people have a tendency of putting their agendas first and then God last. It was not so with Solomon.

But seek ye first the kingdom of God, and his righteousness; and all these things shall be added unto you. (Matthew 6:33)

When your heart and your motives are right, God will elevate you. Solomon was promoted spiritually, and he became a man of great influence and great wealth. Most people will run for power first to secure their position, but Solomon went for God first. Promotion comes from God. When you do first things first you will move from glory to glory.

The method you use when you are building determines whether God will be pleased or not. Take heed to how you build. The Apostle Paul said:

Every man's work shall be made manifest: for the day shall declare it, because it shall be revealed by fire; and the fire shall try every man's work of what sort it is. (1 Corinthians 3:13)

There are two types of builders, those who build with God, for God, and those who build by themselves, for themselves. Solomon was aware of God's intentions. He was not trying to do something that was coming from himself. He did not wake up from a day dream and come up with a crazy idea that said, "I want to construct a building". It was not his idea; he received a vision from God, and through his father. It was his father who wanted at first to build a house for God. But God said, I want your son rather to build me that house.

It was not a struggle for Solomon to complete that task for the following reason: The provision of this building was set aside for him by his father. In other words he did not have to struggle to put everything together all by himself. Why do people struggle today to build that which they claim is from God? Is God not capable of providing for what belongs to Him?

Is it possible that there are people who have claimed certain have come from God, when in actual fact these are ideas or projects of their own conception? While some on the other hand might have claimed to be servants of God, in reality they are not. They might be involved in their own crazy ideas which they claim to be God's vision. When people claim to hear from God why can't He provide for them? Abraham calls Him Jehovah Jireh,

And Abraham called the name of that place Jehovah Jireh: as it is said to this day, In the mount of the LORD it shall be seen. (Genesis 22:14)

God has proved over and over again that He is a God of provision. Abraham's testimony seeks to confirm that on more than one occasion God came through for him.

God has always been known for providing for His own people throughout generations. Our great grandfathers trusted in Him, and even though there were lean and tough times in their generation, God provided for them in new and unexpected ways.

After being led out of captivity in Egypt and into the wilderness, man ate angels' food. God gave them meat from heaven.

He rained flesh also upon them as dust, and feathered fowls like as the sand of the sea. And he let it fall in the midst of their camp, round about their habitations. So they did eat, and were well filled: for he gave them their own desire; (Psalm 78:27-29)

Water from the rock.

Behold, he smote the rock, that the waters gushed out, and the streams overflowed; can he give bread also? Can he provide flesh for his people? (Psalm 78:20)

Their clothes did not tear or wear out for forty years.

Man did eat angels' food: he sent them meat to the full. (Psalm 78:25)

If He is the same God we are serving will He not provide? There is a need to ask this question in our world today, "Where is the God of provision?" Show yourself again Lord, come through for us again Lord like Elisha's prayer…

And he took the mantle of Elijah that fell from him, and smote the waters, and said, Where is the LORD God of Elijah? and when he also had smitten the waters, they parted hither and thither: and Elisha went over. (2 Kings 2:14)

He asked, "Where are you the God of Elijah", maybe we also need to pray, "Where are you the God and father of our Lord Jesus?"

Solomon began to build with God's assistance and he was consistent to the end.

Being confident of this very thing, that he which hath begun a good work in you will perform it until the day of Jesus Christ: (Philippians 1:6)

This is one of the reasons that made it possible for him to finish the construction without complications. He was provided with manpower and everything that he needed by his father.

There is an account in the Bible where Jesus sent His disciples in pairs. He ordered them not to carry extra shoes or food for the journey. He made sure that they were taken care of spiritually and physically.

Upon coming back he asked them a question,

And He said to them, When I sent you without purse and wallet and sandals, did you lack anything? And they said, nothing. (Luke 22:35)

We are apostolically sent by God. Will God who sent us, forget where we are or what we need? Should we not be carrying testimonies just like the disciples of Jesus Christ who saw Satan falling like lightning?

Why is there so much lack today? Why are all these gimmicks, corruption, money games, and monkey games in the body of Chrsit? Oh! There are so many cries concerning the lack of provision for the vision. Whose vision Is It? Is it from God, or from man?

Solomon had all the resources he required to finish his work, and even though his work took a number of years to finish it did not matter. He did not stop half way through for lack of funds. His professional staff did not abandon their work because of lack of payment. Though he was a young man, no destructive force stood in his way on the construction of his father's vision. Indeed his vision became a reality. Why are other visions becoming a nightmare? Is it possible that people can go about saying something in the name of God, when God Himself is hearing it for the first time? Every Godly vision must become a reality. God is a God of provision and there is provision for every Godly vision. He had enough foreign currency to take care of his foreign workers and imported material that was needed for that building.

Upon completion he did not miss the words. He knew exactly who was behind the work he was doing. Going straight to the point, he started by honoring his father by saying, **"it was in my father's heart to build a house for God".** He went ahead to dedicate it to God. In his prayers he pleaded with God to bring down His glory. God responded by coming down in His glory and filling the Temple. Let us not forget that this happened under the Old Testament order. How much more would God do under the New Testament order? God has something to say concerning the New Testament church; that the glory of the latter shall surpass the glory of the former. On the contrary some of the churches today are full of religion and the traditions of man. They lack the glory of God. This question must be asked over and over again, 'Where is the Glory?' It's time for us to pray the prayer of our Lord Jesus who said:

And the glory which thou gavest me I have given them; that they may be one, even as we are one: (John 17:22)

Jesus' prayer was for us to be given the glory that He had. Jesus' glory must be our portion. This is the glory that surpasses the glory of Solomon. The Bible declares that Jesus Christ – and therefore His glory – is in us:

To whom God would make known what is the riches of the glory of this mystery among the Gentiles; which is Christ in you, the hope of glory: (Colossians 1:27)

He is the hope of glory. When His glory comes upon us, His glory is full of grace and truth;

56

And the Word was made flesh, and dwelt among us, (and we beheld his glory, the glory as of the only begotten of the Father,) full of grace and truth. (John 1:14)

Solomon's intentions were clear. He never wanted to get credit for what he knew was not originally his design or plan. He was simply saying, "I want to decrease so that God can increase". It was in this posture that God began to elevate him. When we choose to elevate God He will elevate us. Allow me to quote the words of the greatest scientist who ever lived, Isaac Newton, **"If I have seen farther it's by standing on the shoulders of the giant".** Bernard of charters French Neo-Platonist Philosopher said, **"We are like dwarfs standing or sittings upon the shoulders of giants and so able to see more and see farther than the ancients."**

The reason why we are not seeing that much today is because people have taken upon themselves the sin of self-elevation. This is the same sin that found Lucifer tumbling down from heaven because he disregarded the throne of God and wanted to take God's place. God must be lifted up in everything we do in our lives.

How art thou fallen from heaven, O Lucifer, son of the morning! How art thou cut down to the ground, which didst weaken the nations!

For thou hast said in thine heart, I will ascend into heaven, I will exalt my throne above the stars of God: I will sit also upon the mount of the congregation, in the sides of the north: (Isaiah 14:12,13)

CHAPTER 7

A HOUSE OF PRAYER FOR ALL NATIONS

It does not look like egocentrism was in Solomon's heart when he was building the house his father instructed him to build. It looks like he just wanted to fulfill his father's dream by building a house just as the Bible says,

And said unto them, It is written, My house shall be called the house of prayer; but ye have made it a den of thieves. (Matthew 21:13)

Let me also suggest that Solomon was a people's person, whose mind was motivated by people's needs. He was very passionate about where his people were going to worship. His focus was not personal it incorporated the community of worshipers that would benefit from this building, that was the passion behind his vision. His main focus was to build a house which was going to bring all the praises and the glory to God. He was indeed establishing a spiritual center where humankind would come and communicate with their Creator, a World Outreach Center that bore his father's signature, his wisdom and vision. His ultimate goal was to have a "glory" house for God where God's people would bless their God and be blessed. The model and main concern of his ministry was that he may be a blessing to all God's people.

For every high priest taken from among men is ordained for men in things pertaining to God, that he may offer both gifts and sacrifices for sins: (Hebrews 5:1)

Solomon was ordained from man, for man, to God; he was indeed a true minister of God's people who represented the needs of the people to God without any self-centeredness in his service to God's people. The Temple he built can be compared to a "one stop" shop where one can find everything he needs, a complete package so to speak. A closer look at his prayer clearly indicates what was in his heart.

O generation of vipers, how can ye, being evil, speak good things? For out of the abundance of the heart the mouth speaketh. (Matthew 12:34)

The day he prayed this prayer he was representing the needs of the people before God the Father. His concerns were clear as an open book before God.

And now, O God of Israel, let thy word, I pray thee, be verified, which thou spakest unto thy servant David my father. (1 Kings 8:26)

In his lengthy prayer he pleaded with God as he presented almost everything line upon line and precept upon precept.

He sincerely asked God to verify and to vindicate His word that He spoke to his father David. You could hear that Solomon wanted more than just a Temple; he wanted God's manifestation to be seen in the Temple, and a visible manifestation of the prophetic word that came from God through his father's mouth. He requested God to honor his prayer and to put His eyes upon the Temple that he had built. He cried earnestly and asked God to watch over that house. This shows the caliber of his leadership. He was a leader full of discernment for the needs of his people, their difficulties and the challenges that were among them. He sought to resolve these issues in the Temple he had built.

He fully comprehended the principle that every natural problem finds its origin in the spiritual realm. He knew if there can be a spiritual place that can address their spiritual struggle their spiritual state would consequently improve their lives. To him the value of the Temple was not in its beauty or the cost. The looks did not mean much. Solomon wanted a place that would minister to God's people in a variety of ways. Hence he began to list things that he expected God to take care of and he said, when the people come to pray in this place because of sin may they be forgiven.

And hearken thou to the supplication of thy servant, and of thy people Israel, when they shall pray toward this place: and hear thou in heaven thy dwelling place: and when thou hearest, forgive. (I Kings 8:30)

He longed for to see people's sins forgiven in that Temple; a house of forgiveness. He had a full understanding that people can sin against God and this place could serve as a sanctuary where people could access mercy and forgiveness. This house had multiple functions that dealt with various issues his subjects had to navigate in real life. He prayed that God would come through and completely meet the needs of the people. He recognized that if the people sinned it could cause a national calamity; therefore he took the initiative and lead Israel in a prayer of repentance. He understood that he had to take a proactive leadership role in order for the needs of the people to be met in the house of God. Solomon was indeed a purpose-driven leader whose prayer echoed almost every need of his people and the will of God for His people.

He said to God, when neighbors are in conflict may this be a place of judgment and reconciliation. He sought God on behalf of the people that God may come through for them. He did not overlook the times when the enemies may come and strike them. So part of his request was that the resident anointing in that Temple should provide for vengeance against their enemies.

Indeed his prayer was an "all-rounder"; he did not forget to mention sicknesses, diseases, famine, and all sorts of natural disasters that may try to affect God's people. Thinking to the future, he prayed that when the heavens are shut down and there is no rain may the supplications offered in this place cause the heavens to open and bring rain. It was a house of healing, and a house of an open heaven for rain to come down. A house where curses would be broken and burdens lifted. The diversity of the anointing that was resident in that house was capable of taking care of every need that might arise.

Foreigners or strangers from other nations were not left out on his prayer list. Concerning the strangers that would come to the house of God he asked that they be blessed. Yes, it was indeed the house of strangers, and a house of victory and a house where both locals and visitors were all welcome. This house was to touch everyone from all walks of life; a true picture of what the church of Jesus Christ is all about.

THE HOUSE OF DELIVERANCE

The house that Solomon built was also a house of deliverance. God is our deliverer. He is our shield and our fortress.

And he said, The LORD is my rock, and my fortress, and my deliverer; The God of my rock; in him will I trust:he is my shield, and the horn of my salvation, my high tower, and my refuge, my saviour; thou savest me from violence. I will call on the LORD, who is worthy to be praised: so shall I be saved from mine enemies. (2 Samuel 22:2-4)

The word "deliverance" is quite an interesting word. Let us look at it for a moment. Deliverance means rescue from captivity, hardship, or domination by evil.

I would like to believe that the time David spent with his son was quality time. They might have used this time to go through all the details of how the Temple was going to be laid out, its purpose and its spiritual mission. I would like to believe that deliverance was high on the agenda. That deliverance of God's people was found in the Temple as part of the blessed package. Indeed God is our deliverer, and He rescues us from hardship or evil domination. It was not just a magnificent building that he wanted to build; it was more than a building.

Any ministry that focuses on the outside beauty and not on how it can impact the people of God is nothing but an idol... and God forbids idolatry. In my experience on the mission field, as I travel the nations of the world, I have been to places where some people who had come in the name of missions have left a lot to be desired and did more harm than good. When I tried to find out about the impact of their mission, I came to discover that some of the missionaries in some places have not done a genuine work, but rather they were promoting their own agendas. After doing my own enquiry from some of the regular church members, I came to the conclusion that most of them had no knowledge of salvation, or had no clue of what's going on. They were just blind followers of "someone" who came in the name of a missionary. There is a popular saying concerning missionaries who went to Africa motivated by greed and self- enrichment, "If you want to be rich go to Africa." There are missionaries who gather a lot of native people together and take photographs of them and start raising funds to advance their own greed. Solomon was different. He wanted and pursued the deliverance of God's people. It is important to ask yourself, What is my motive? Are you motivated by God or gold?

CHAPTER 8

THE HOUSE OF PROPHECY: A ZION TEMPLE

And the LORD appeared to Solomon by night, and said unto him, I have heard thy prayer, and have chosen this place to myself for a house of sacrifice. If I shut up heaven that there be no rain, or if I command the locusts to devour the land, or if I send pestilence among my people; If my people, which are called by my name, shall humble themselves, and pray, and seek my face, and turn from their wicked ways; then will I hear from heaven, and will forgive their sin, and will heal their land. Now mine eyes shall be open, and mine ears attend unto the prayer that is made in this place. (2 Chronicles 7:12 -15)

The Temple of Solomon indeed became what his father David dreamt of a place where God's name would dwell. God himself said this is going to be my dwelling place. Allow me to call it a "house of prophecy". God spoke to Solomon concerning this house, saying that He had chosen it and made it holy. He assured Solomon that He was going to dwell in that house and that the prayers that were going to be made in this house were going to affect God's decisions. Thus to say when people had fallen into sin there was going to be diseases and famine. When people would come into this house God would pardon and hear them. He also made it exclusive for His people. Whenever God's chosen people would come in and pray in this house He would hear them.

It was a fulfillment of prophecy that God gave to David concerning his son. In other words it was a fulfillment of number of prophecies, including the one that was given to David, in which God was speaking prophetically concerning the future generations that would frequent that house. It was indeed a house that was built and borne from divine inspiration that was to become a center for all the nations of world. God confirmed this by saying He had honored that house and had accepted the prayers that had been offered, including those that were going to be offered in the future. He even mentioned that this house would be a symbol of answered prayers, that even from a distance when people prayed facing that direction, God would hear and answer them. This house was honored and sanctified by God so much that it was like God's headquarters on earth. People did not need to be in the Temple to be heard by God. Even if people had traveled a long distance away from the epicenter of the Temple, they were guaranteed answered prayer when they prayed facing that direction. God said, "I will hear their prayers and I will heal their land."

The vessels in that Temple continued to speak prophetically when they were taken into Babylon many years after Solomon had departed from the earth… and many years still after the original prayer was made.

The king of Babylon took a vessel and used it to drink wine; Belshazzar, whiles he tasted the wine, commanded to bring the golden and silver vessels which his father Nebuchadnezzar had taken out of the Temple which was in Jerusalem; that the king, and his princes, his wives, and his concubines, might drink therein. Then they brought the golden vessels that were taken out of the Temple of the house of God which was at Jerusalem; and the king, and his princes, his wives, and his concubines, drank in them. They drank wine, and praised the gods of gold, and of silver, of brass, of iron, of wood, and of stone. In the same hour came forth fingers of a man's hand, and wrote over against the candlestick upon the plaister of the wall of the king's palace: and the king saw the part of the hand that wrote immediately the hand of God began to write on the wall. (Daniel 5:2-5)

This was many years after Solomon had dedicated the house of God. The vessels were so anointed that whosoever touched them would be affected by the power of the prayers that dedicated them. It is of vital importance to note that whatever is dedicated to God becomes God's. Do not misuse the vessels dedicated to the work of God. The people around you, peers and your fellow man are created in the image of God. Misusing and abusing them can result in the judgment of God over your life.

Know ye not that ye are the Temple of God, and that the Spirit of God dwelleth in you? (1 Corinthians 3:16)

If the vessel that was in Solomon's Temple caused God to intervene and write the message on the wall how much more would He intervene on those whose lives were purchased by the blood of His Son Jesus Christ? When Solomon prayed his prayer many years before that prayer was still valid and active when these vessels were found in Babylon. Anything that is dedicated to God must be treated with double honor. Anything that is dedicated to God carries God's glory, His presence and His protection. Indeed the Temple that Solomon built was a prophetic center. After the completion of the dedication he called for a seven day nonstop celebration. The number seven stands for perfection and completion.

And on the seventh day God ended his work which he had made; and he rested on the seventh day from all his work which he had made. (Gen 2:2)

We are the latter day church. We are living in the 21st century; a generation that is expected to live in the complete and perfect glory of God. We are a Zion church that worships God joyfully just as it was in the Temple of Solomon. People rejoiced and they were fed for seven days. We are the latter day church that is better than the former. Paul speaks of vessels when he said,

If a man therefore purge himself from these, he shall be a vessel unto honour, sanctified, and meet for the master's use, and prepared unto every good work. (2 Timothy 2:21)

We are truly the vessels of honor that God has sanctified to speak prophetically. We are just like the vessels that spoke prophetically in Babylon. We have been built to be the habitation of God in the spirit.

In whom ye also are built together for a habitation of God through the Spirit. (Ephesians 2:22)

Even as the Bible says we are the Temple of the Holy Spirit, a house of prayer for all God's people where God reveals and speaks to His people, a place of prophetic declaration.

CHAPTER 9

FAVOR AND PROSPERITY

Solomon successfully built that which was in his heart through God's favor, and he prospered. When God is on your side nothing can withstand you. As the scripture below declares it is God who gives you power to get wealth.

And they rose early in the morning, and went forth into the wilderness of Tekoa: and as they went forth, Jehoshaphat stood and said, Hear me, O Judah, and ye inhabitants of Jerusalem; Believe in the LORD your God, so shall ye be established; believe his prophets, so shall ye prosper. (2 Chronicles 20:20)

I strongly believe that prosperity comes from God. In the case of Solomon there is no doubt that the reason he prospered was that the Lord God gave him the power to prosper.

But thou shalt remember the LORD thy God: for it is he that giveth thee power to get wealth, that he may establish his covenant which he sware unto thy fathers, as it is this day. (Deuteronomy 8:18)

The leadership mantle that was on his father's life was transferred to him. When some members of his family were coveting the same leadership position, they could not get it because he had favor with his father, the prophet, his mother and the priest. The day he was put into power all these people were present wishing him prosperity and success.

And let Zadok the priest and Nathan the prophet anoint him there king over Israel: and blow ye with the trumpet, and say, God save king Solomon. (1 Kings 1:34)

They were all present on the day when honor was transferred to him, and on that very day I would like to believe that the anointing of prosperity was set in motion. He continued to grow from strength to strength. He had favor with everyone, including the neighboring kings. His entire reign was marked by peace. His government was organized with uniqueness and his administration was admired by all. He prospered physically, spiritually, naturally and territorially. Let us take a closer look at Solomon and the way he gave his offerings.

GIVING LIFESTYLE

And King Solomon offered a sacrifice of twenty and two thousand oxen, and a hundred and twenty thousand sheep: so the king and all the people dedicated the house of God. (2 Chronicles 7:5)

From this statement we can see that Solomon was a man of great substance. No one can give that much unless he has been blessed with much. As the Word of God declares, to whom much is given much will be required.

For unto whomsoever much is given, of him shall be much required: and to whom men have committed much, of him they will ask the more. (Luke 12:48)

A single offering from Solomon was a true reflection of how strong he was financially.

HIS WEALTH

And she gave the king a hundred and twenty talents of gold, and of spices great abundance, and precious stones: neither was there any such spice as the queen of Sheba gave king Solomon. And the servants also of Huram, and the servants of Solomon, which brought gold from Ophir, brought algum trees and precious stones. Now the weight of gold that came to Solomon in one year was six

hundred and threescore and six talents of gold; Beside that which chapmen and merchants brought. And all the kings of Arabia and governors of the country brought gold and silver to Solomon. And king Solomon made two hundred targets of beaten gold: six hundred shekels of beaten gold went to one target. And three hundred shields made he of beaten gold: three hundred shekels of gold went to one shield. And the king put them in the house of the forest of Lebanon. Moreover the king made a great throne of ivory, and overlaid it with pure gold. And there were six steps to the throne, with a footstool of gold, which were fastened to the throne, and stays on each side of the sitting place, and two lions standing by the stays: And twelve lions stood there on the one side and on the other upon the six steps. There was not the like made in any kingdom. And all the drinking vessels of king Solomon were of gold, and all the vessels of the house of the forest of Lebanon were of pure gold: none were of silver; it was not anything accounted of in the days of Solomon. For the king's ships went to Tarshish with the servants of Huram: every three years once came the ships of Tarshish bringing gold, and silver, ivory, and apes, and peacocks. And king Solomon passed all the kings of the earth in riches and wisdom. And all the kings of the earth sought the presence of Solomon, to hear his wisdom, that God had put in his heart. And they brought every man his present, vessels of silver, and vessels of gold, and raiment, harness, and spices, horses, and mules, a rate year by year. And Solomon had four thousand stalls for horses and chariots, and twelve thousand horsemen; whom he bestowed in the chariot cities, and with the king at Jerusalem. (2 Chronicles 9:9-25)

CHAPTER 10

THE SONS IN THE BIBLE AND THEIR BENEFITS

THE BENEFITS OF SON-SHIP

When we take a closer look at some of the sons in the Bible we will find a lot of examples that will teach us a great deal as we study the lives of those that have been here before us. We will discover how both biological and spiritual sons interacted with their fathers.

LESSONS FROM THE PAST

There are indeed many lessons relevant for our day to day life that are able to teach us how we can position ourselves in order to relate with our biological and spiritual fathers whom God has placed above us. Everything that happened in the past has some great lessons for us to learn from. History has a lot to teach us, which requires a study of the past. The Bible explains the benefits of looking to the past for direction in the future:

For whatsoever things were written aforetime were written for our learning, that we through patience and comfort of the Scriptures might have hope. (Romans 15:4)

The cited scripture seeks to address that history has a lot to teach us and that includes the subject of fathers and sons. The father and son relationship is a kingdom and a biblical principle. Indeed if you look through the Bible there are powerful examples that everyone can learn and benefit from. The father and son relationship is part of what forms the kingdom of God. The Bible speaks about the God of Abraham, Isaac and Jacob, and by just observing that we see continuity of the father and son relationship from Abraham, Isaac to Jacob.

70

Aaron and his sons are also another very good example of priestly ministry that came out of a father and his sons. God ordained Aaron and his sons to be in the priestly ministry.

Bring your relatives of the tribe of Levi to assist you and your sons as you perform the sacred duties in front of the Tabernacle of the Covenant. (Numbers 18:2 NLT)

Let us take another observation of Abraham and his son Isaac:

And in thy seed shall all the nations of the earth be blessed; because thou hast obeyed my voice. (Genesis 22:18)

The story of Isaac and Abraham began with God giving a promise to Abraham that he was going to have a son - that son was destined to release the blessings to the entire world. It was through him that all the nations of the world were going to be blessed. God had deposited all the blessings of the world in this one son. Parallel to this earthly relationship, God has His heavenly kingdom and in His kingdom He has a Son. All blessings come through His son. No one can access God's throne, His mercies or love outside His Son:

Jesus saith unto him, I am the way, the truth, and the life: no man cometh unto the Father, but by me. (John 14:6)

When God gave Abraham the promise He was replicating what He has in His heavenly kingdom here on earth. The name "Isaac" means he "laughs" or he "laughed". Scholars have debated the question of who is laughing. If God is implied the name could indicate divine amusement at an aged couple ridiculing the prospects of having a child. God has a Son...His one and only Son. He spoke to Abraham declaring that he was going to have a son, and through this son God was extending his family on the earth. And it was through that son that God was going to have many sons on the earth.

For whom he did foreknow, he also did predestinate to be conformed to the image of his Son, that he might be the firstborn among many brethren. (Romans 8:29)

Isaac came into the life of his parents in their old age. I believe that he enjoyed certain benefits that come with being the child of promise. Abraham raised him up in the ways of God remembering the covenant he had with God, and instructed Isaac in the role that he was going to play as a son. He equipped him with the vision making him aware of his overall duties and what God expected of him. It is written that God gave Abraham a mandate to teach his children His ways. Some of the lessons he was going to teach his son was how to worship and offer sacrifices to God, and also to live and walk by faith. God told Abraham to go to the Mount Moriah. Upon communicating this to his child, Isaac did not refuse because he was raised to be familiar with this kind of worship. He was familiar with the kind of worship and the relationship that his father had with God, his Father. Children must know the God of their fathers. The younger generation needs to be taught how to connect with God. When children are properly taught even going to church does not become a challenge or problem. Isaac could not say "no" when he was asked to come along for a time to worship God. He came along fairly aware of all what they were going to do, as he understood how his father worshiped from a young age. This is confirmed by the fact that he even asked the father where the sacrifice was;

And Isaac spake unto Abraham his father, and said, My father: and he said, Here am I, my son. And he said, Behold the fire and the wood: but where is the lamb for a burnt offering? (Genesis 22:7)

This suggests that he knew what materials were needed for worship. A well taught son is not stubborn, destructive, or a hindrance in times of worship. Rather he is supportive and compliments the process and always plays his part. He did not try to argue it out; all he did was to remind his father about the elements that were needed for worship in case he had forgotten to choose a choice ram for an offering to God.

They went on a three day journey to a place of worship, and all the while there was no complaint from Isaac. When he asked his father where the offering was his father did not explain everything at once, neither did he tell him where the offering was. His answer was that God would provide. These were the words of Jesus to his disciples;

I have yet many things to say unto you, but ye cannot bear them now. Howbeit when he, the Spirit of truth, is come, he will guide you into all truth: for he shall not speak of himself; but whatsoever he shall hear, that shall he speak: and he will shew you things to come. (John 16:13)

A father only reveals the necessary information to his son on a "need to know" basis, because he has insight and understanding of where his son is spiritually, psychologically and socially. A father is familiar with all the levels of growth in his child, and therefore only releases to him only what he can handle at the time. He gave him an answer that indicated divine provision. This confirms that Abraham had taught his boy some faith principles that included the supernatural provision of God's hand. He gave him an honest and faithful answer, even though he knew that God meant Isaac himself was the sacrifice. It is important to note that when God initially communicated to Abraham, the message was for Abraham, not his son. Therefore it was improper for Abraham to reveal to Isaac what was not meant for his ears. A true father knows what to conceal and what to reveal, when to hold back and when to release. If God had told him to tell Isaac what the Lord had in store, the order of events would have looked very different. Some people don't know what to say and when to say it. You must not say what you are not supposed to say unless God orders you otherwise. Permit me to say that Abraham did not tell Isaac all the details regarding the sacrifice because he was to be the actual sacrifice.

Upon arriving at the place of worship Isaac had no clue about what God had spoken to his father. When they arrived at the place of worship his father tied him and placed him on the altar. Isaac had complete trust in his father. He was not moved neither did he complain.

He just lay there like a sheep to the slaughter and spoke no word. He had complete trust in his father's actions. Physically, he was strong enough to overpower Abraham… but there is no suspicion and fear in a father son relationship. It is a relationship that hopes for the best. He was an obedient child, just as Jesus Christ was and became obedient even unto death;

And being found in fashion as a man, he humbled himself, and became obedient unto death, even the death of the cross.   Wherefore God also hath highly exalted him, and given him a name which is above every name: (Philippians 2:8 — 9)

Solomon had a similar experience on account of his obedience, faithfulness, endurance and patience. Those qualities yielded certain dividends at the end of the day. When a son walks in the footsteps of his father he will not miss the heavenly blessings. As the word of God declares:

Honour thy father and thy mother: that thy days may be long upon the land which the LORD thy God giveth thee. (Exodus 20:12)

Isaac did not struggle even when the time came for him to get married. He did not try to figure out where to find Miss Right. His father was fully involved and gave his son instructions on where and how to find a suitable bride – one who would bring him comfort.

And I will make thee swear by the LORD, the God of heaven, and the God of the earth, that thou shalt not take a wife unto my son of the daughters of the Canaanites, among whom I dwell: (Genesis 24:3)

But thou shalt go unto my country, and to my kindred, and take a wife unto my son Isaac. (Genesis 24:4)

And Isaac brought her into his mother Sarah's tent, and took Rebekah, and she became his wife; and he loved

her: and Isaac was comforted after his mother's death. (Genesis 24:67)

God our father knows who will make us happy, and cause us no grief, and bring us true comfort. It is important to involve God our heavenly Father in every choice we make, and every move we make, if we are going to live a life full of happiness. His wife came from the same village as his mother. Abraham enjoyed the relationship with his wife and he thought that if his son would get married, it must be someone with his mother's qualities, including her beauty. Ironically, one could argue that the only flaw in that relationship was Sarah's good looks, since it caused Abraham problems wherever he went with his wife. If we follow the life of Isaac, we will discover that somewhere along the way he picked up similar challenges as his father because of his wife's beauty.

There is further indication that Isaac was a carrier of his father's vision. He also re-dug Abraham's wells, pointing to the fact that he was physically (and fiscally) committed to his father's "trade", so to speak. In spite of the opposition and resistance that he faced from the Philistines who tried to stop him from re-digging the wells, he still managed to reassign them the original names that his father had given them.

And Isaac dug again the wells of water, which they had dug in the days of Abraham his father; for the Philistines had stopped them after the death of Abraham: and he called their names after the names by which his father had called them. (Genesis 26:18)

He was just continuing with his father's vision, carrying on from where his father had left off and he did not get side tracked or discouraged until the opposition gave up on him.

And he removed from thence, and digged another well; and for that they strove not: and he called the name of it Rehoboth; and he said, For now the LORD hath made room for us, and we shall be fruitful in the land. (Genesis 26:22)

His father's inspiration made him a great man of vision and leadership. He began to flow in his father's anointing and blessings due to his submission and obedience that he demonstrated.

FAMILIAR THINGS OF TRUE SONS

SONS OF THE PROPHETS

Let us go, we pray thee, unto Jordan, and take thence every man a beam, and let us make us a place there, where we may dwell. And he answered, Go ye. And one said, Be content, I pray thee, and go with thy servants. And he answered, I will go. So he went with them. And when they came to Jordan, they cut down wood. But as one was felling a beam, the axe head fell into the water: and he cried, and said, Alas, master! For it was borrowed.

And the man of God said where fell it? And he showed him the place. And he cut down a stick, and cast it in thither; and the iron did swim. (2 Kings 6:2 – 6)

You may note that this scripture has an interesting subject regarding the sons of the prophet. Similarly if a comparison was to be made, there are some common themes that are interwoven together throughout the Bible as it relates to the subject of fathers and sons. There are indeed similar things that stand out as uniform. The word "uniform" simply means: unchanging, always the same, in the quality, degree character of manner, consistent conforming to one standard, resembling one another or others. If you look at the account of the sons of the prophets you would agree that there is resemblance of what we discussed early on in other passages of this book. The way the sons of the prophets related with Elisha is no different from the way that anyone would relate with his father. This passage deals with the subject of a relationship of a spiritual father and his sons. It was a dialogue pointing out that their dwelling could no longer accommodate their number and requesting permission to relocate to a bigger and better location. They held a proper consultation with their father with regard to their vision. They brought a crystal clear vision that was very broad and submitted it to their father. Vision is a clear mental picture of a preferable future. The sons of the prophet wanted a future that looked much better than their present state. Vision becomes a starting point as well as the intended end.

They sought to improve and develop what they already had and they knew where they were heading. Everyone with a vision has a beginning and knows exactly where they want to end. Having observed all spiritual protocol, they had a clear understanding that in order for them to achieve success there must be proper communication with their father because it was absolutely essential and vital.

So they told their spiritual father of their intention to build with their ultimate goal being the acquisition of a better place for all to stay. It was therefore crucial for them to submit the vision first to their father before attempting to do anything. They operated in a team spirit and never did anything as individuals hence the saying, **"let us go we pray thee and take hence every man a beam**." The term "let us go" denotes the fact that it was not a "one man band". They had a specific location where they wanted to go. Their father's accompaniment was crucial in this matter. All their success depended on it.

Their father's back up support was indeed an absolute necessity. The physical and spiritual presence of their father determined whether they were going to make it or not. Those that make it in life are those that consult their fathers before they take off. Your pre-trip study is essential. Your enquiry of how long the journey will be and how you get there is absolutely necessary to determine whether you will get there or not. Hence they needed a green light in order for them to get to their bigger and better space. When the mission was approved by their father they asked once more if he would go with them. When they finally accessed the approval and the blessings of their father, they got the confirmation that he was going to be with them. I would like to believe that he saw their genuineness, their vision and their willingness to go all the way. They had the heart to work. Their mission was not for themselves but to benefit everyone. Their motives were right; they sought their father's blessings and they were all willing to play a part for the completion of the building.

They said, "We will do the work… just be with us." All they needed was his company. They did not want to go alone. They were simply saying we need your presence. There is something about being in the company of people of influence and high authority. Rubbing shoulders with them releases a high motivation and a rush of excitement, let alone the ability that makes it possible for one to finish the work. The presence of a spiritual father can change and charge one's ability to complete the impossible. In the case of the sons of the prophets, even though they had their blessings and the company of their father, something still went wrong. Upon commencing with the cutting of the beams for the construction of the building there was an unexpected occurrence that took place. They lost their axe.

But as one was felling a beam, the axe head fell into the water: and he cried, and said, Alas, master! for it was borrowed. (2 Kings 6:5)

It came to their remembrance that among them was a servant of God - more than the servant of God - their own spiritual father. His involvement played a major role in bringing about a resolution to the problem in that hour. They pleaded for him to help locate the axe that went missing and he agreed to help, miraculously recovering the axe to their amazement. Are there things missing in your life? Are you in the right company, missing the right covering? When the axe went missing he did not put the blame on them, or criticize them by unnecessarily questioning them as to why they used borrowed equipment instead of using their own. Rather he went straight to recover the axe so that they could go on with their work. Who are you with: Are you with those that help you to recover or build you up when you are down?

Solomon's father's instructions were the keys to his building construction. Along with them were best wishes and blessings that were accompanying him all the way to success. On the other hand Isaac was accompanied by the blessings because he followed his father's vision in obedience and without grumbling even in times when it did not make any sense. He went along with his father to a place of worship where God had ordered him to go. The sons of the prophets under the divine instruction of the father recovered the axe.

"And David enquired at the LORD, saying, Shall I pursue after this troop? shall I overtake them? And he answered him, Pursue: for thou shalt surely overtake them, and without fail recover all."(I Samuel 30:8)

David had a predicament and enquired in prayer to his heavenly father by asking the following question: "Can I go and will You help me to be victorious?" The reason he was enquiring whether to go or not was because he wanted some divine instructions. If you study the life of David throughout you will come to the conclusion that these references were familiar in his life. He had an awareness of the power that was in divine instruction, hence he sought God for the green light. This was an incredible loss in his life. He had lost everything including his wives, children and the wives and the children of his colleagues who were in his army.

It was during that time that he knew that his life depended only on one voice; he knew that if he went because God told him to go it would make a difference. The question that may be asked is, "What was he doing when he lost his family?" David engaged himself in something that was none of his business, and it resulted in his loss. It was during in his absence when the enemy came and took everything away including his wives and children. It is very costly to be found at a place where you are not supposed to be. It may result in a devastating loss. That's how we come to realize that it is even more costly to be outside the will of God. One good thing about our God is when we ask Him about anything He is always there to give us the answer. Note: this was a definite answer with a full assurance that he will recover all. Be assured before you go! David got a prophetic assurance; he was also told the pace he was going to need to complete this task. It was by means of overtaking.

Overtaking is to be better than somebody or something; to come over somebody suddenly or to get someone by surprise. Overtaking also speaks of speed. God's speed and divine acceleration made it possible for David to recover all. When God comes through for anyone apostolically or prophetically the outcome will be a complete turnaround. God's word declares that "He gives us the desires of your heart."

Delight thyself also in the LORD; and he shall give thee the desires of thine heart. (Psalm 37:4)

Jesus said all the power has been given to me He gives you the ability to do a complete work he has all the power;... Jesus came and spake unto them, saying, All power is given unto me in heaven and in earth. (Matthew 28:18)

There is a place in God where He allows you have complete blessings, not partial blessings. He is a God of a complete package. He wants us to have abundant life.

The thief cometh not, but for to steal, and to kill, and to destroy: I am come that they might have life, and that they might have it more abundantly. (John 10:10)

He wants us to have no lack. In David's case these people were in distress because they had lost their families. He also lost his family and was troubled. When we study this scenario we will come to the conclusion that these were the results of a bad decision. A closer study on where David was prior to this condition indicates that he had gone to some place where he was not supposed to be in the first place. He was out of place and out of timing and it cost him so dearly. Being out of place is dangerous and it may cost you everything that you have. Every leader's subjects are totally dependent on his decisions; therefore he bears a greater responsibility to carefully consider the results of his choices and actions.

There are people today that God has placed under your spiritual care and they depend on your prayers. Failure to pray for them may bring indescribable tragedies upon them. Therefore it is important to correct one's wrongdoing like David, who sought God when he had done wrong. He went to God in repentance as he sought for directions and instructions as to how he could recover from his loss. On the other hand his people were speaking of stoning him.

One might ask, "Why people were speaking of stoning him?" The answer would be, there was sin in play in David's life; the sin of engaging into something without God's directives. Never engage yourself in something that does not have God's complete assurance or approval for. Yes it is possible that when we don't enquire from God we open ourselves to unnecessary confrontations. Thank God for David's lesson because it teaches us that he had to go through a time of repentance even as his prayer confirms. He enquired from the Lord; he sought for divine direction and instruction. Don't build alone. You will be building in vain. Build with God and you will build successfully. Build with God and you will build in deed. Solomon wrote these powerful words;

Except the LORD build the house, they labour in vain that build it: except the LORD keep the city, the watchman waketh but in vain. (Psalm 127:1)

He received a prophetic word and an apostolic release to go. God gave him a specific agenda to overtake his enemies. He went with God's speed. God's power was upon him, he overtook and recovered all.

CALEB AND JOSHUA'S RELATIONSHIP

Then the children of Judah came unto Joshua in Gilgal: and Caleb the son of Jephunneh the Kenezite said unto him, Thou knowest the thing that the LORD said unto Moses the man of God concerning me and thee in Kadeshbarnea. Forty years old was I when Moses the servant of the LORD sent me from Kadeshbarnea to espy out the land; and I brought him word again as it was in mine heart. Nevertheless my brethren that went

up with me made the heart of the people melt: but I wholly followed the LORD my God. And Moses swore on that day, saying, Surely the land whereon thy feet have trodden shall be thine inheritance and thy children's forever, because thou hast wholly followed the LORD my God. And now, behold, the LORD hath kept me alive, as he said, these forty and five years, even since the LORD spake this word unto Moses, while the children of Israel wandered in the wilderness: and now, lo, I am this day fourscore and five years old. As yet I am as strong this day as I was in the day that Moses sent me: as my strength was then, even so is my strength now, for war, both to go out, and to come in. Now therefore give me this mountain, whereof the LORD spake in that day; for thou heardest in that day how the Anakims were there, and that the cities were great and fenced: if so be the LORD will be with me, then I shall be able to drive them out, as the LORD said. And Joshua blessed him, and gave unto Caleb the son of Jephunneh Hebron for an inheritance. Hebron therefore became the inheritance of Caleb the son of Jephunneh the Kenezite unto this day, because that he wholly followed the LORD God of Israel. (Joshua 14:1-14)

The story of Caleb and Joshua is about a father and a son. Their story is marked by many spiritual adventures that they both undertook while they were under the leadership of Moses, the servant of God. They were part of the original group that left Egypt through the mighty delivering hand of God, when God sent Moses to deliver the children of Israel and bring them to the land of the promise. These two undertook an assignment to go and spy the land and upon coming back there was a great prophecy that was released concerning Caleb.

This scripture in Joshua is a confirmation of what had taken place when Caleb was forty years of age and had received a prophecy from Moses, the servant of God. This prophecy was concerning his blessings and the real estate that was to be his. However it took forty-five years for this prophecy to be a reality. It is believed that Caleb was a foreigner who became part of what God was doing and God established him among His chosen people. He was a great and humble man who understood spiritual protocol, and he operated in great faith while following the Lord whole-heartedly. The scripture declares that because Caleb wholly followed the Lord, God was well pleased to assure him the perpetual inheritance. **"....Surely the land shall be thine inheritance."**

As Caleb's story shows us, inheriting one's blessings is no mere walk in the park. It took forty-five years for this word to be manifested, according to Caleb's own testimony when he said, "the Lord has kept me alive". When God's word is spoken it produces life.

Jesus said my word is spirit and life; It is the spirit that quickeneth; the flesh profiteth nothing: the words that I speak unto you, they are spirit, and they are life. (John 6:63)

However in the life of Caleb there is a lesson to be learnt. Even though he had received a word from Moses, the servant of God, it was going to take a proper observation of spiritual protocol in order for that word to be manifested. I don't want to say that it took forty-five years before this word could be manifested. It is possible that the delay was because Caleb did not initially observe spiritual protocol. In my own suggestion I would like to say it was only when Caleb acknowledged Joshua as his spiritual father then was this word activated. Indeed there must be a spiritual father over one's life through whom all the spiritual blessings of God can flow. In this case God had spoken through Moses, but now Moses was no longer there.

Joshua was now Moses' successor and Caleb came to remind him of the forty-five year old prophecy. Through his acknowledgement and submission he went ahead and reminded the man of God of what God had spoken through Moses, and that he was looking forward to seeing that word coming to pass. He told Joshua that he was feeling young and requested to be given his mountain that God had given to him through prophecy. If God was with him he would be able to drive the Anakim out of the land as the Lord said. In other words he fully acknowledged the one who now had a spiritual mandate over his life. He sought for the blessings and the release to go ahead in the name of the Lord God. And the word of God declares Joshua blessed him.

The man who waited forty-five years now he had the key to his blessings and was equipped to fight the Anakims. The Anakims were giants; the great grandfathers of Goliath. Though Caleb was old, he refused to succumb to notions about his advanced age and charged into battle. As the old saying says, "you are as old as you feel". He declared I feel forty! Age does not matter. It is the Word of the Lord that is important; the communicated word in addition to the blessings of the father that will bring a turn around. He got his inheritance. **"....Kirjatharba and Aba was the great king among the Anakims was taken over by Caleb and it became Hebron."**

In spite of his background he inherited what God spoke through the mouth of his fathers. Find your father and your blessings will follow you.

JOSEPH

HIS NAME

Joseph was the son of Jacob. The name Joseph means "the Lord will add" and it was a very common name in biblical times. Even though there are many Joseph's in the Bible there is one Joseph whose story stands out, the son of Jacob. Despite many difficult circumstances and contending with evil people, Joseph remained true to God and was generous to other people. As a result God made him extremely successful and used him to save the whole Hebrew race.

FAVOR

Favor was his portion. He was highly favored by his father. There is nothing comparable with the favor of the father. His connection with his father positioned him in a place of God's blessings. He came into his father's life in the eleventh hour. He was the eleventh child of his old age. Joseph was loved and highly favored; he carried the blessings of the eleventh hour. There are benefits of walking in the father's love and favor. His father declared him the first born, even though genealogically this was not factual. Joseph had older brothers, born from a mother who Jacob had been tricked into marrying.

But when Jacob woke up in the morningwas Leah! "What sort of trick is this?" Jacob raged at Laban. "I worked seven years for Rachel. What do you mean by this trickery?" (Genesis 29:25 NLT)

Jacob never stopped loving Rachel (his one intended wife) and after Joseph was born, he viewed him as the true first born and gave him the blessing and love of that position that made his other brothers hate him. There is nothing like the father's love. It opens doors both spiritually and otherwise. His love will always be there and provides the best at all times. For his part, Joseph proved to be trustworthy and a man of integrity - unlike his other brothers. After carefully studying his life you discover that he was someone who was true, steadfast, and God fearing.

He was a hard working shepherd. In other words he took care of business and his father could count on him. As he became the father's favorite more duties were delegated to him - more than his brothers, and as a result they became increasingly jealous of him. On the other hand he began to receive heavenly visions regarding his future leadership. The Interpretations of those dreams pointed to him in an exalted position, and this is something his brothers could not agree with.

He grew up and became a fine leader. His father was a good judge of character. He saw the potential in the life of his fine son. He connected with him more because of his obedience. His father began to spoil him and bought him a coat of many colors which symbolized royalty and apostolic leadership. That created even more hatred from his brothers. One day his father sent him to go and check on his brothers. He was obedient to do as his father commanded, even though he knew the tension that existed between him and his brothers. When he reached his brothers they decided to get rid of him once and for all. This was the beginning of another long road of tribulation and intensive hardships. When his brothers returned home they lied to their father, telling him Joseph was dead. His father cried bitterly for he was his favorite son.

And Jacob rent his clothes, and put sackcloth upon his loins, and mourned for his son many days. (Genesis 37:34)

And all his sons and all his daughters rose up to comfort him; but he refused to be comforted; and he said,

For I will go down into the grave unto my son mourning. Thus his father wept for him. (Genesis 37:35)

When people try to get rid of you don't be worried; the Father's love will sustain you. Joseph's father's tears were not just tears. Allow me to say those were prayers to God.

Leadership is not just a position, but influence. And even in the house of bondage Joseph's gift of leadership shined through. In the midst of hardship Joseph stood out. True sons are not those that give in to pressure. Pressure and hardship only makes them better. Joseph endured hardships because he knew what destiny God had in store for his life and he knew that his father was counting on him. The wickedness in his brother's hearts did not have any impact on him. Rather, he decided to be different as he was more concerned in preserving the family name. Sons that are concerned about the future will not play with fire, for they are thinking generationally. God finally brought him to the throne. He reconciled him together with his family and he began to address his brothers as he gave them the interpretation of their betrayal, using these words:

As for you, you meant evil against me, but God meant

it for good in order to bring about this present result, to preserve many people alive. (Genesis 50:20)

His calling to leadership had a long term blessings and provision for every family member. This may mean that his father did not make a wrong choice; he had insight for the better tomorrow. Hence he bestowed favor and honor upon him.

In another situation God ordered Moses to ordain Joshua and put some honor upon him.

Now Joshua the son of Nun was filled with the spirit of wisdom, for Moses had laid his hands on him; and the sons of Israel listened to him and did as the LORD had commanded Moses. (Deuteronomy 34:9)

JOSHUA

Joshua was a true son in the ministry of Moses, and served Moses until God decided to promote him. Promotion comes from God and not from man. True sons are those that perfect their jobs until they become overqualified for that work. It is then that they are given bigger and more challenging tasks. Joshua never took part in any rebellious activities, he carried out his spying mission and he remained true to his father even among ten spies. He came out among those who had the most positive report. He was also among the troop that was sent from Cadesh Barnea from the tribe of Ephraim who were instrumental in the defeat of the Amalekites. He was instrumental in the defeat of the Amalekites where Moses built an altar and called that place the "Lord is my Banner." (Genesis 17:8 - 15)

In the ministry of Moses, Joshua fully functioned as a son as even the heavens testified. The Amalekites were defeated under the leadership of Joshua, and God ordered Moses to write that testimony down as a reminder to him. It was already clear at this point that God was raising him up as the future leader of His people. Moses changed his name to Joshua as seen in the scripture below.

These are the names of the men which Moses sent to spy out the land. And Moses called Oshea the son of Nun Jehoshua. (Numbers 13:16)

The Hebrew name Yehoshu'a (Joshua), means YAWHEH is salvation which means Jehovah is salvation.

When Moses sent spies out from Cadesh Barnea, Joshua and Caleb were the only two who came back with the positive report about the land. Allow me to say that Joshua was a positive son who was full of faith, who believed every word God spoke concerning the children of Israel. He believed that they would conquer and possess the Promised Land. Upon his impending death, Moses asked God about his successor. God revealed to him that Joshua was the man for the job.

And Moses spake unto the LORD, saying, Let the LORD, the God of the spirits of all flesh, set a man over the congregation, Which may go out before them, and which may go in before them, and which may lead them out, and which may bring them in; that the congregation of the LORD be not as sheep which have no shepherd. And the LORD said unto Moses, Take thee Joshua the son of Nun, a man in whom is the spirit, and lay thine hand upon him; And set him before Eleazar the priest, and before all the congregation; and give him a charge in their sight. And thou shalt put some of thine honour upon him, that all the congregation of the children of Israel may be obedient. (Numbers 27:15 - 20)

Upon Moses' death the leadership of Joshua was confirmed.

These are the names of the men which shall divide the land unto you: Eleazar the priest, and Joshua the son of Nun. (Numbers 34:17)

Joshua, the anointed warrior, was now in full leadership over the children of Israel and was now ready to take over Jericho. The anointing of his father Moses was now active in his life and the similar miracles that were in Moses' life were active in his. Just as his father crossed the red sea, Joshua crossed the river Jordan.

And it came to pass, when all the people were clean passed over Jordan, that the LORD spake unto Joshua, saying, Take you twelve men out of the people, out of every tribe a man, And command ye them, saying, Take you hence out of the midst of Jordan, out of the place where the priests' feet stood firm, twelve stones, and ye shall carry them over with you, and leave them in the lodging place, where ye shall lodge this night. (Joshua 4:1)

Joshua performed mighty miracles, including causing the walls of Jericho to fall. Even though he was one of the oldest people to enter the promise land, Joshua was given the city he asked for: Timnath'serah, in the hill country Ephraim.

When they had made an end of dividing the land for inheritance by their coasts, the children of Israel gave an inheritance to Joshua the son of Nun among them: According to the word of the LORD they gave him the city that he asked for, "even Timnathserah in mount Ephraim: and he built the city, and dwelt therein."

Joshua is a true picture of what a son with unfailing faithfulness should do and he charged the people of God to continue serving the Lord faithfully. All Israel served the Lord under the leadership of Joshua. He a man renowned for this famous speech:

And if it seem evil unto you to serve the LORD, choose you this day whom ye will serve; whether the gods which your fathers served that were on the other side of the flood, or the gods of the Amorites, in whose land ye dwell: but as for me and my house, we will serve the LORD. (Joshua24:15)

Joshua kept his faith to the end. He was a strong warrior who fought to the end just like Paul who said,

I have fought a good fight, I have finished my course, I have kept the faith. (2 Timothy 4:7)

Joshua was known for conquering the land of Canaan. Unlike Moses who only saw it from the distance, Joshua tasted the milk and the honey. He was known for being a great assistant to Moses. It was a true father and son relationship. Joshua and Caleb were faithful, brave and courageous sons. Finally he walked in the footsteps of his father and had a flow of his anointing. God was so pleased with him that he gave him the mantle of his father.

ABEL AS A SON

Most sons observe and learn from their father's ways. Let us take a look at the life of Abel as he imitated his father.

And Abel, he also brought of the firstlings of his flock and of the fat thereof. And the LORD had respect unto Abel and to his offering. (Genesis 4:2)

As Abel practiced what he had learnt it brought upon him some tremendous blessings. It is contained in the Bible that the honoring of parents has indeed some blessings that it brings. Adam was the son of God and he was told what to do in order for him to abide in the blessings of his Father. When he fell short in the Garden of Eden he started improvising by making religious routines that were empty. Man in his sinful condition cannot resolve anything pertaining to sin.

When sin is in place there is only one way to deal with it and that way is traced back to God. Only God can forgive sin. What is sin? Sin is the breaking of the law or missing the mark, it is selfish rebellion against God's authority. When sin has been committed only God can pardon, forgive, and restore. Adam tried to work out his own salvation by his own means. This became the introduction of the law of works.

He employed physical labor as means of getting out of sin, by cutting down some fig leaves in an attempt to cover his sin.

Even though he knew that the fig leaves would soon dry up, he continued to cut them down to provide for his covering. Our works can only cover us temporarily, their profit is minimum, and they can never provide absolute results. In order for God to be God He must know everything. Being fully aware of what Adam had done, God came to implement certain principles to resolve Adam's case. Before God could implement those principles He wanted to first establish his location. God was more interested in his spiritual location than physical. God will not give you anything unless you know where you are spiritually. It will be improper for us to say God did not know where he was because in order for God to be God He must know everything. The reason Adam was hiding was because of his sin. The immediate results of sin are shame and guilt, which result in one going into the closet.

However God's requirement was to know what Adam's response was. Adam responded defensively. Meanwhile, God was not seeking his defense, rather his accountability. Nevertheless, Adam did not face up to his responsibility by admitting his fault. His response should have been, "I blew it". I compromised Your authority; I questioned your instructions therefore my wife and I decided to eat from the tree that you forbade us to eat from." He did not ask for forgiveness. He rather blamed his wife for all that had gone wrong. He took cover and hid himself, and yet even in that state God still came to give him a few lessons on how to come out of sin.

God gave him a practical demonstration by slaughtering an innocent animal. It is written in the scripture that without the shedding of the blood there is no remission of sins.

And almost all things are by the law purged with blood; and without shedding of blood is no remission. (Hebrews 9:22)

God took away the life of an innocent animal because life is in the blood.

For the wages of sin is death; but the gift of God is eternal life through Jesus Christ our Lord. (Romans 6:23)

The consequence of what Adam committed was a death penalty, so God was saying only death was going to provide forgiveness of sin. For the first time an animal had to die as a substitute for man's sins. After learning this lesson Adam began to exercise this type of worship that was to be followed throughout all generations. This symbolized what God was going to do in the fullness of time, He was going to send His Son, who was going to die as a Lamb of God to take away the sins of humankind.

However, before the Lamb of God came, animals were speaking prophetically and symbolically about what was coming. As a son, Abel observed his father's way of worship and followed it through, when he came to worship God not only did he bring an animal for sacrifice but he also brought the first fruit.

He came to worship God with the first born of his animals, and the Lord was pleased with him. Adam, God's son, passed on what was taught to him by God to his son. Adam's other son Cain, on the other hand did not put into practice what he was taught by his father. He ended up bringing an illegitimate offering that was not accepted by God, thereby missing the blessings of God.

If thou doest well, shalt thou not be accepted? (Genesis 4:7)

Only God's ways bring happiness. Jealousy got hold of him and he ended up killing his brother, Abel, as a result. Consequently, Cain became the first murderer on the earth and he was cursed perpetually.

God's blessings and covering are the best. Adam came to realize that fig leaves can only last for a moment before they dry. God provided him with real leather clothing that was intended for longevity. It covered him for a long time and it was the best outfit that he could ever get. The father's love is real and not fake. When you do what is right you will be established. Cain became a wonderer because he did not follow his father's footsteps. Abel was justified; even after he was murdered his blood still spoke. Are you following your father in worshipping God in spirit and in truth or have you become a wonderer?

CUSHI AS A SON IN JOAB'S ARMY

Now Absalom in his lifetime had taken and reared up for himself a pillar, which is in the king's dale: for he said, I have no son to keep my name in remembrance: and he called the pillar after his own name: and it is called unto this day, Absalom's place. Then said Ahimaaz the son of Zadok, Let me now run, and bear the king tidings, how that the LORD hath avenged him of his enemies. And Joab said unto him, Thou shalt not bear tidings this day, but thou shalt bear tidings another day: but this day thou shalt bear no tidings, because the king's son is dead. Then said Joab to Cushi, Go tell the king what thou hast seen. And Cushi bowed himself unto Joab, and ran. Then said Ahimaaz the son of Zadok yet again to Joab, But howsoever, let me, I pray thee, also run after Cushi. And Joab said, Wherefore wilt thou run, my son, seeing that thou hast no tidings ready? But howsoever, said he, let me run. And he said unto him, Run. Then Ahimaaz ran by the way of the plain, and overran Cushi. And David sat between the two gates: and the watchman went up to the roof over the gate unto the wall, and lifted up his eyes, and looked, and behold a man running alone. And the watchman cried, and told the king. And the king said, If he be alone, there is tidings in his mouth. And he came apace, and drew near. And the watchman saw another man running: and the watchman called unto the porter, and said, Behold another man running alone. And the king said, He also bringeth tidings. And the watchman said, Me thinketh the running of the foremost is like the running of Ahimaaz the son of Zadok. And the king said, He is a good man, and cometh with good tidings. And

Ahimaaz called, and said unto the king, All is well. And he fell down to the earth upon his face before the king, and said, Blessed be the LORD thy God, which hath delivered up the men that lifted up their hand against my lord the king. And the king said, Is the young man Absalom safe? And Ahimaaz answered, When Joab sent the king's servant, and me thy servant, I saw a great tumult, but I knew not what it was. And the king said unto him, Turn aside, and stand here. And he turned aside, and stood still. And, behold, Cushi came; and Cushi said, Tidings, my lord the king: for the LORD hath avenged thee this day of all them that rose up against thee. And the king said unto Cushi, Is the young man Absalom safe? And Cushi answered, The enemies of my lord the king, and all that rise against thee to do thee hurt, be as that young man is. (2 Samuel 18:18 —32)

This is another example of a father and son relationship. Joab was a commander in David's army. As a chief general in the army, part of his duty was to delegate work to his troops according to their ranks. One would say he was a father to those that were under his command. The above scripture tells us of an incident that had taken place during a confrontation of a rebel army which resulted in Absalom's death. An informant by the name Ahimahaz came to the commander Joab and requested to go and give the breaking news.

He wanted to run to the royal house and tell the king. Joab as a commander refused him that opportunity, telling him that you are not going to get the news today but another day. Then Joab said to Cushi, "Go and tell the king what you have seen." And Cushi took off and ran. The commander communicated to another news reporter because in this particular situation this news was classified. It involved the death of the king's child, or specifically a report of the murder of the king's child. As a father Joab gave a command to Cushi. Every assignment must be communicated from the top to the bottom. I have maintained this point throughout the passages of this book - that everything flows from the communicated word. The father releases a word and that word carries a blessing and it guarantees success for the vision thereof. The news was to reach the king and it was classified information. The king's child was dead and someone needed to take the news and break the news in such a way that was diplomatic and less offensive.

And how shall they preach, except they be sent? as it is written, How beautiful are the feet of them that preach the gospel of peace, and bring glad tidings of good things! (Romans 10:15)

One must be given a mandate and the blessings from someone superior or with authority before they embark on a journey. Even the devil understands spiritual protocol. The classic story of the sons of Scheva illustrates this point. This scripture seeks to teach that no one must do a spiritual work without a mandate because it can only lead to humiliation or to total failure. What happened in this case resulted in them being undressed by the people who were possessed by evil spirits preceded by qualifying questions which they could not answer.

And the evil spirit answered and said, Jesus I know, and Paul I know; but who are ye? (Acts 19:15)

What a pity some people want to do some spiritual work without a divine mandate. One may ask under whose authority do they operate from? The spiritual world understands spiritual positions and ranks even in the dark world, as we have noticed in the example of the children of Sceeva in the cited scripture. Cushi - under the leadership of Joab - was an imaginative news reporter... but he did not take off without being given the marching orders. You'll find in this story that he was inexperienced. He was not a swift runner, but when Joab said go to the royal house, he knew that word carried everything that he ever needed to complete the task he was given. Covered by the blessings of his commander he was sent to speak to the king. He did this under the protection of his father and that was a guarantee that he was going to be received by the king.

One of the 'professional reporters' appeared and also demanded to go and give the breaking news. And General Joab said not this time Ahimahaz; you will go some other time. I have sent somebody else and I have blessed him. However he insisted because he was so used to doing this sort of task and he still wanted to go even though he did not have a detailed report for the king. Upon insisting, he was released to go. And although Ahimahaz arrived before the amateur reporter Cushi, he could not communicate accurately due to his lack of information. David knew him, he was a well-known reporter with a good reputation who could run fast, however in this case he did not have full details of what had transpired.

It's not how well qualified or accurate one is; it's all about whose mandate one is under. Sons who run with a mandate may not be experienced, however the covering and the blessings they receive from their father gives them credibility, accuracy and details. They don't fall short; they reach their destiny and deliver without fail. Upon arriving, King David received Cushi's message and the message was very clear. Unlike the experienced reporter, who upon arriving could not flow. There are two types of people in the world today: Those that are sent and have a proper relationship, a spiritual covering and a spiritual father, and those that are self-sent, self-enthroned, and independent. The latter is a Luciferian spirit who sought to be like God, taking upon himself responsibilities without accountability. The sons that are sent by their father have a prolific way of delivery. Cushi was carrying the bad news that the king's child was no more.

However his method of delivery was not offensive, he did not ridicule the victim, or implicate any one as a cause of death. Wisdom was in his speech he understood diplomacy. He even showed the king that it was the Lord who had brought the war to an end. He knew the language of the king. He spoke what I call "kinglish". He knew how to speak with the authorities in a diplomatic manner. Allow me to say he ran with the message and with father's blessings: the commander in chief, Joab. When he was received by the king, he was not a self-sent but rather went where he was sent to go. That allowed him to complete his diplomatic mission with honor, without disgracing himself like the sons of Sceva who were humiliated for lack of spiritual mandate and vision.

Who are you running with? Under whose covering are you? Run with the father and you will reach your destiny.

TIMOTHY AS A SON

On his journey, Paul met with Timothy whose mother was a Jewess - and a believer - but whose father was a Greek.

Then came he to Derbe and Lystra: and, behold, a certain disciple was there, named Timotheus, the son of a certain woman, which was a Jewess, and believed; but his father was a Greek: (Acts 16:1)

Paul decided to include Timothy in his trip as one of his disciples because people spoke well of him. Timothy became Paul's son and joined him in the work God gave to Paul. Paul circumcised Timothy for the sake of doing the work effectively as Jewish people were expected to go through circumcision. Timothy was not obligated to be circumcised because he was Greek. However he agreed with Paul by obeying him when he approached him with the idea of circumcision. This was an act of submission to his father. Timothy did not doubt his spiritual father for what he was doing. He knew the God of Paul and the zeal Paul had for the work of God.

So he sent into Macedonia two of them that ministered unto him, Timotheus and Erastus; but he himself stayed in Asia for a season. (Acts 19:22)

The time came where Timothy was left to look after the church in Ephesus. Paul was busy with his apostolic journey, continuing with vision of impacting the nations. There is no way Paul could have given Timothy this responsibility if he had not qualified as a son. When Paul writes to Timothy he opens his letter by saying:

To Timothy, my true child in the faith: Grace, mercy, and peace from God the Father and Christ Jesus our Lord. (1 Timothy 1:2)

A responsible son is the crown of glory to his father. Proper communication was the key to Timothy's success in the ministry. He also had a heart to labor; he put every effort to the advancement of God's work. Doing requires effort and effort leads to labor, labor leads to finished work,

Thou therefore, my son, be strong in the grace that is in Christ Jesus. And the things that thou hast heard of me among many witnesses, the same commit thou to faithful men, who shall be able to teach others also. Thou therefore endure hardness, as a good soldier of Jesus Christ. (2 Timothy 2:1-3)

REIGN WITH HIS FATHER

As I mentioned earlier on, the father and son relationship is not self-centered. He became a successful pastor because of his commitment and submission to the vision that God had given to his father, and as a result he became well recognized and honored everywhere he went. Oftentimes he was sent to undertake missions on behalf of Paul, his father, and his father recommended that he be received without contradiction. His maturity and ability gave his father the confidence that he could represent him in a worthy manner. Timothy was a son who was building on nothing else but the instructions of his spiritual father- Paul.

I charge thee before God, and the Lord Jesus Christ, and the elect angels, that thou observe these things without preferring one before another, doing nothing by partiality. (1 Timothy 5:21)

He became one of the most successful leaders of his time. He enjoyed the benefits of son-ship as he was charged to raise many sons.

And the things that thou hast heard of me among many witnesses, the same commit thou to faithful men, who shall be able to teach others also. (2 Timothy 2:2)

SAME FLOW WITH HIS FATHER

When Timothy joined Paul, he did not come with a list of his own rules, but rather submitted to the leadership of Paul at all cost. He respected the man of God as his father. He submitted to the instructions Paul gave him for the ministry. A father and son relationship is not a self-centered relationship, whereby a father is serving his own interests while on the other hand, the son is pursuing his own agendas. The vision became the focal point and the center of attraction for both. What Paul experienced in ministry he in turn passed it on to his son. Paul was a champion of scriptures and he had a strong background of sound doctrine and a rich study life. He studied under the best theologian of his time, Gamaliel. He encouraged Timothy to study the scriptures, to teach and to preach, watching his life and doctrine closely.

Study to shew thyself approved unto God, a workman that needeth not to be ashamed, rightly dividing the word of truth. (2 Timothy 2:15)

Sons are responsible for and active in their father's business; they take care of it as if it were their own. Paul had complete confidence in his spiritual son because he shared with him the same apostolic grace. Also Paul reproduced himself in Timothy and gave him encouragement and instructions concerning the ministry and leadership. It is so sad today that we hear of so many spiritual sons being the cause of division, taking members and starting their own churches without a proper release by their fathers. Timothy traveled with Paul learning in preparation for the work that was ahead of him. It takes proper preparation to work the works of God effectively. One must be completed submitted to the effort of preparation. "There is no spiritual promotion without spiritual preparation".

There was a unique grace that Timothy needed in order for him to flow with Paul his father. He needed to tap into it by way of impartation through the laying on of hands from his father, Paul.

Wherefore I put thee in remembrance that thou stir up the gift of God, which is in thee by the putting on of my hands. (2 Timothy 1:6)

Paul released the impartation upon his son Timothy. He also gave him the divine strategy of how to fight the good fight of faith.

This charge I commit unto thee, son Timothy, according to the prophecies which went before on thee, that thou by them mightest war a good warfare; (1 Timothy 1:18)

Sons are protected under the father's covering and they are given divine strategies of warfare in the apostolic ministry.

TIMOTHY WAS A SON

Paul says,

For though ye have ten thousand instructors in Christ, yet have ye not many fathers: for in Christ Jesus I have begotten you through the gospel. (1 Corinthians 4:15)

Paul - speaking to the Corinthian church - was trying to make them understand the importance of spiritual fathering. Spiritual fathering is a biblical order which provides spiritual accountability as seen throughout the Bible. Aaron's ministry was a father and son ministry, the Levites were the sons of Aaron.

And take thou unto thee Aaron thy brother, and his sons with him, from among the children of Israel, that he may minister unto me in the priest's office, even Aaron, Nadab and Abihu, Eleazar and Ithamar, Aaron's sons. (Exodus 28:1)

Noah's ministry was with his sons.

Then Noah and his sons and his wife and his sons' wives with him entered the ark because of the water of the flood. (Genesis 7:7)

He and his sons were the only people who survived the flood when God destroyed the whole world. Abraham's ministry was with his son.

David's ministry was with his son. God finished the work of the cross through His Son. Spiritual fathering therefore provides a ministry base and a prophetic presbytery. Paul says to Timothy,

Neglect not the gift that is in thee, which was given thee by prophecy, with the laying on of the hands of the presbytery. (I Timothy 4:14)

In his book Presbytery and Apostolic Teams, John Eckhardt gives a detailed account of the order of the Presbytery.

"The presbytery at Antioch consisted of prophets and teachers who ministered to the Lord and fasted. From this group Barnabas and Saul were chosen by the Holy Spirit and sent out to minister.

Let us define the word presbytery; the word presbytery appears once in the New Testament in I Timothy 4:14. The Greek word is "presbuterion" which means the order of elders. Presbytery is a group of elders that make up the government of the local church.

This verse gives us at least two characteristics of local elders. The presbytery should be able to minister prophetically and they should be able to lay hands and impart. Timothy received the gift through the laying on of hands and prophecy. The presbytery is the key to imparting and releasing strong ministry gifts."

Paul as a spiritual father to Timothy was encouraging him and reminding him that he should not neglect the gift that was imparted to him through a group of fathers who formed a presbytery and ministered to him prophetically. In other words he was saying there was a prophetic gathering of fathers who laid hands on you as a witness to your calling, don't allow anything to make you doubt that.

As I said earlier on, fathers are to provide for divine accountability. In times of doubt and fear they will be there. In the case of Timothy he was going through a challenge and Paul was writing to him in reference to the ministry of the presbytery that ministered to him in the days that had gone by. Fathers are those that will speak to you and strengthen you when you are going through difficult times. That is why Paul was saying you have many instructors but not many fathers. A father is more than an instructor. He is someone before whom you can be naked to and be transparent and they will provide a spiritual covering as was in the life of Paul and Timothy.

Paul and Timothy ministered together; your father can be your co-minister.

And there accompanied him into Asia Sopater of Berea; and of the Thessalonians, Aristarchus and Secundus; and Gaius of Derbe, and Timotheus; and of Asia, Tychicus and Trophimus. (Acts 20:4)

They traveled together and planted churches together yet Paul called Timothy,

Unto Timothy, my own son in the faith: Grace, mercy, and peace, from God our Father and Jesus Christ our Lord. (1 Timothy 1:2)

Timothy had a prophetic presbytery that ministered to him and imparted to him, and released prophetic utterances regarding his gift. Paul and Barnabas were ministered to at the church in Antioch by a prophetic presbytery that released a prophetic word concerning their ministry.

We see a similar picture here on the seventh day when Jesus was being dedicated to the Lord. God allowed Simeon, a man who feared God and who had a prophetic grace upon his life, to come in and prophetically release a word over Jesus. Anna the prophetess was present and she also prophesied.

And, behold, there was a man in Jerusalem, whose name was Simeon; and the same man was just and devout, waiting for the consolation of Israel: and the Holy Ghost

was upon him. And it was revealed unto him by the Holy Ghost, that he should not see death, before he had seen the Lord's Christ. And he came by the Spirit into the Temple: and when the parents brought in the child Jesus, to do for him after the custom of the law, Then took he him up in his arms, and blessed God, and said, Lord, now lettest thou thy servant depart in peace, according to thy word: For mine eyes have seen thy salvation, Which thou hast prepared before the face of all people; A light to lighten the Gentiles, and the glory of thy people Israel. And Joseph and his mother marvelled at those things which were spoken of him. And Simeon blessed them, and said unto Mary his mother, Behold, this child is set for the fall and rising again of many in Israel; and for a sign which shall be spoken against; (Yea, a sword shall pierce through thy own soul also,) that the thoughts of many hearts may be revealed. And there was one Anna, a prophetess, the daughter of Phanuel, of the tribe of Aser: she was of a great age, and had lived with a husband seven years from her virginity; And she was a widow of about fourscore and four years, which departed not from the Temple, but served God with fastings and prayers night and day. And she coming in that instant gave thanks likewise unto the Lord, and spake of him to all them that looked for redemption in Jerusalem. (Luke 2:25 — 38)

Dr. Bill Hamon in his book Prophets, Pitfalls and Principles says:

"Prophetic Presbytery is when two or more prophets and/or prophetic ministers lay hands on and prophesy over individuals at a specified time and place".

Prophetic presbyteries are conducted for several reasons.

1. For revealing a church member's membership ministry in the body of Christ.

2. For ministering a prophetic rhema word of God to individuals.

3. For impartation and activation of divinely ordained gifts, graces and callings.

4. For the revelation, clarification and confirmation of leadership ministry in the local church.

5. For the "laying on of hands and prophecy" over those called and properly prepared to be a five-fold minister. (unquote)

Paul - as a spiritual father to Timothy - encouraged him and instructed him to study the word of God.

Study to shew thyself approved unto God, a workman that needeth not to be ashamed, rightly dividing the word of truth. (2 Timothy 2:15)

He also instructed him to avoid religious politics and vain debates. He basically provided checks and balances over his life in the ministry.

But watch thou in all things, endure afflictions, do the work of an evangelist, make full proof of thy ministry. (2 Timothy 4:5)

This scripture is dealing with the three-fold aspect of fatherhood. Paul is advising vigilance in all things. In other words, he was saying observe, take a look and don't take everything for granted. Our Lord Jesus says in the book of Luke 26:41 to watch and pray. There is a need for daily examination to make sure whether you are still on the cutting edge. There is nothing like self-deception to make you think you are still standing while you have already fallen. That is why Paul was saying check your prayer life observe all things.
Examine yourselves, whether ye be in the faith; prove your own selves. Know ye not your own selves, how that Jesus Christ is in you, except ye be reprobates? (2 Corinthians 13:5)

In 1 Peter 5:8, Peter speaks about something similar noting that one needs to be sober and vigilant because there is an enemy out there. That is why spiritual fathering is so crucial.

Paul went on to say "…do the works of an evangelist make full proof of your ministry." As a father, Paul knew exactly what Timothy was called to do. Thus he encouraged him to make sure he fulfilled his calling and election. He was not expecting him to fall short but to make full proof of his ministry. True fathers will not fight with your ministry and will not compete with your ministry, but will complement you to make sure you become what God wants you to be. He went on to finalize his instructions by saying endure hardship as a good soldier of Christ. There is a war out there and fathers are those who have been involved in the battle and would not want you to be misled by thinking it's an easy walk but would want you to be strong and face the enemy. The book of John 16:33 declares that in the world we shall have tribulations.

These things I have spoken unto you, that in me ye might have peace. In the world ye shall have tribulation: but be of good cheer; I have overcome the world. (John 16:33)

We face opposition on a daily basis. That is the reason why you need to stand with some heroes of the faith who have seen, fought and won some battles. Who will give you some hints and clues of how to win this war? Thank God for spiritual fathers.

JESUS AS A SON

THE FATHERS LOVE

We were once children of disobedience, living under the wrath of God as the word of God declares;

Among whom also we all had our conversation in times past in the lusts of our flesh, fulfilling the desires of the flesh and of the mind; and were by nature the children of wrath, even as others. (Ephesians 2:3)

We were "aliens" regarding the things of God. We were not a people, we were dying without hope and without God in our sins as it is stated:

Which in time past were not a people, but are now the people of God: which had not obtained mercy, but now have obtained mercy. (I Peter 2:10)

All of creation was under Adamic sin. By one man's deeds, sin entered the whole world,

For as by one man's disobedience many were made sinners, so by the obedience of one shall many be made righteous. (Romans 5:19)

God created man in His own image and placed him in the Garden of Eden. He commanded him not to eat the tree of the knowledge of good and evil, warning that if he did he would he would be ex-communicated. Man disobeyed God through the wife who listened to the deception of the serpent who enticed her to eat of the forbidden fruit. God's love and mercy caused Him not to totally abandon man after his fall. Instead He offered him a plan of salvation and redemption as seen in the passages below. The following scripture spoke prophetically about the complete redemption of the fallen man that would come through the seed of the woman.

And I will put enmity between thee and the woman, and between thy seed and her seed; it shall bruise thy head, and thou shalt bruise his heel. (Genesis 3:15)

In other words there was going to be a reset, similar to the one of the First Adam. God was bringing the Last Adam who was going to be born of a virgin and who was going to take upon Himself the sins of all mankind. He was going to bruise the head of the serpent, which speaks of judgment to the serpent who was the root cause to the fall of the first Adam.

For unto us a child is born, unto us a son is given: and

the government shall be upon his shoulder: and his name shall be called Wonderful, Counsellor, The mighty God, The everlasting Father, The Prince of Peace. (Isaiah 9:6)

The reset was going to bring a rebirth to a regeneration of the fallen man through Jesus the Christ, God's Son, who was going to be the first born among many who were going to be kin with Him and would form the family of God on the earth.

For whom he did foreknow, he also did predestinate to be conformed to the image of his Son, that he might be the firstborn among many brethren. (Romans 8:29)

But as many as received him, to them gave He power to become the sons of God, even to them that believe on his name. (John 1:12)

He was going to be the only way through whom the whole creation was going to be reconciled back to God. According to the book of Romans;

For you did not receive the spirit of slavery to fall back into fear, but you have received the Spirit of adoption as sons, by whom we cry, "Abba! Father! (Romans 8:15)

When Christ comes into one's life He re-establishes the broken relationship between him and God. It is through Christ alone that we become sons of God. One can only be a son of God through Jesus. Jesus taught in the Lord's Prayer that man ought to pray to our Father who art in heaven.

It is interesting to note that Christ came to reconcile the entire world back to God so that they may become part of the household of God in the earth as it is in heaven. The Scripture declares,

Behold, what manner of love the Father hath bestowed upon us, that we should be called the sons of God: therefore the world knoweth us not, because it knew him not. (1 John 3:1)

God has a Son in heaven… His only begotten son. What He has in heaven He also wants to see here on earth. So God sent His Son to be the first born among many brethren that through Jesus He may have many sons on earth. Upon arriving He even taught that people should pray for the will of God to come on earth as it is in heaven.

And he said unto them, When ye pray, say, Our Father which art in heaven, Hallowed be thy name. Thy kingdom come. Thy will be done, as in heaven, so in earth. (Luke 11:2)

Those that are in Christ Jesus become Jesus' younger brothers. This subject is not about male or female :when you are in Christ you become a son, whether or not you are a male or female. In the spiritual realm there is no gender. In Christ we are all sons of God. The examples that I have used in this book do not seek to discriminate against females because in the spiritual realm all are sons. In the kingdom of God male and female will function in peace. We all have received the spirit of adoption whereby we cry "Abba father". It is through Christ that we are able to say to God "Father" once again. It is through Christ that we get our birthright, which enables us to communicate to God as sons. Those that receive Jesus are given power to become the sons of God. Our coming into Christ was foreknown by God.

For whom he did foreknow, he also did predestinate to be conformed to the image of his Son, that he might be the firstborn among many brethren. Moreover whom he did predestinate, them he also called: and whom he called, them he also justified: and whom he justified, them he also glorified. (Romans 8:29 —30)

God wants us to be conformed to the image of His Son. In the beginning God said let us make man in our own image. Adam had the image of the Son of God before the fall. This was God's original intention: for man to be like Him. God wants us to go back to that image of His own son and the process He has employed to achieve that is through His only Son our Lord Jesus Christ.

And Jacob called unto his sons, and said, Gather yourselves together, that I may tell you that which shall befall you in the last days. (Genesis 49:1)

Similarly the Bible says,

For the earnest expectation of the creature waiteth for the manifestation of the sons of God. (Romans 8:19)

Jacob ordered his sons to come together as he was going to reveal to them that which was to take place in the last days. Jacob, functioning as a type of prophet was revealing the future to his sons. We are living in the most interesting times and these times will be signified by what God had in His original plan.

The original purpose of God creating man on earth was so that man can represent his kingdom on the earthly realm. Man with God's attributes, image and His authority. Even after Adam failed, God had a plan B to bring man back so that he could continue where Adam failed. The first Adam failed, but the world is about to see the manifestation of the last Adam. The first Adam was the son of God who manifested God on the earth. He had the fullness of His glory. It was God's pleasure for him to function in that position until sin was found in him. However, after his fall the prophetic word came to him saying there was another Adam coming. The last Adam was going to be God's Son, Jesus. He was going to restore the first Adam and he was not going to fail.

And so it is written, the first man Adam was made a living soul; the last Adam was made a quickening spirit. (I Corinthians 15:45)

The Bible declares that He gave the fivefold ministry,

For the perfecting of the saints, for the work of the ministry, for the edifying of the body of Christ:[13] Till we all come in the unity of the faith, and of the knowledge of the Son of God, unto a perfect man, unto

the measure of the stature of the fullness of Christ: (Ephesians 4:12, 13)

The whole purpose of the fivefold ministry is to bring the body of Christ into maturity, until we all come to the fullness of the stature of Jesus the Christ. God is building His church to become a complete representation of His Son on the earth. Jesus is the head and the church is the body. Indeed the world is waiting for the full manifestation of the sons of God. We are living in the interesting days where we are going to see the demonstration of the supernatural power of God through those who are kin with Jesus. He predicted that the day was coming where greater works were to be done through the saints. Indeed the saints of the Lord will take the Kingdom and will reign forever more.

But the saints of the most High shall take the kingdom, and possess the kingdom forever, even for ever and ever. (Daniel 7:18)